until
infinity

ROSA LEE JUDE

Printed in the United States of America

ISBN-10:1-942994-04-4
ISBN-13:978-1-942994-04-6

Rosa Lee Jude

Visit my website at www.RosaLeeJude.com

BOOKS BY ROSA LEE JUDE

Contemporary Romance
I STILL DO

Urban Fantasy
The Enchanted Journey Series:
TREMBLE
JASMINE
NEVERWRONG

Time Travel/Historical Fiction
The Legends of Graham Mansion Series:
(with Mary Lin Brewer)
REDEMPTION
AMBITION
DECEPTION
SALVATION
REVELATION

until
infinity

before

Chapter One

"DEARLY BELOVED, WE ARE GATHERED here today in the presence of these witnesses, to join Jared and Lana in the bonds of holy matrimony."

Jared gazed into Lana's eyes as the minister stated their vows. Jared knew he should be listening intently to what was being said, but Lana's eyes were distracting him. The deep pools of green, almost grass green, were like a field into forever. Those eyes were diverting his attention on the most important day of his life. That, and the bug that was crawling on his foot. Jared was not afraid of bugs in general. It was just here they stood in a small old chapel, in a remote corner of the college campus where they had first met, and Jared had no idea what type of bug had just crawled over his foot and up his pant leg. His feet were firmly planted on a pine floor that was over two hundred years old. There was no telling what kind of bugs could creep from between the floor slats.

Lana was dressed in a gorgeous formal gown. He was dressed in a hot tuxedo. They were the picture perfect couple, except for one thing. They didn't have any shoes on. That summed up their romance. That was his Lana.

To some, it might have seemed like a strange request. To Jared, it made perfect sense. Lana had spent days going from one bridal boutique to another looking for her dream wedding gown. She had finally chosen a stark white one that hugged her body with hundreds of tiny beads and sequins. It was a conventional look for her traditional side. That was the same part of her personality that chose law as her career. Not wearing shoes with the expensive gown screamed the side of her that was by far Jared's favorite. Lana's free spirit was stubborn like concrete and adventurous like a kite. It was a crazy intoxicating combination that had captured his whole heart from the very first time they spoke to each other. Jared did not care what they were wearing as long as he got to marry the girl of his dreams. He would, however, desperately like to kill that bug.

The itchy feeling must have taken his thought process away from the words being spoken to him. A tug on his hand from his bride brought Jared back to the present. The minister was staring at him with a questioning look on his face.

"I do." Jared enthusiastically spoke the standard wedding line.

"Yes, Jared. You have already said that." A roar of laughter travelled through the guests. Jared could feel his mouth getting dry. He felt his leg involuntarily shake to try and get the bug off. This incited more laughter from the congregation of family and friends. "It's time for you to repeat after me."

Looking back at Lana, Jared gave her a nervous smile. She squeezed his hand, but the expression in her eyes told him he would have to explain what had distracted him during their wedding ceremony. Jared took a deep breath and moved his attention away from her eyes. Hanging around her neck was a reminder that this day was merely a formality—a public expression of what they had already privately vowed. The pendant she faithfully wore each day symbolized a bond even stronger than the bands of gold they were about to add to their fingers. These vows would make their love legal, an example of the traditional. Lana and Jared had pledged eternity to each other a long time ago.

"FOREVER, MY DARLING—."

"That's got to be our song."

"What song?" Jared kept working on his statistics homework as he questioned Lana.

"That song that is playing right now. It plays every time we come here. Listen to the words, it's talking about infinity."

"*Forever burn——.*"

"Umm, it sounds like Elvis. That would be about right for Mr. Luigi's tastes. I don't think that there are any living singers on that jukebox of his. I guess that's why you don't have to pay to listen to them."

Jared's joking response did not satisfy Lana. She slid out of their corner booth and headed for the jukebox. It was not exactly the type of song you would expect to find on a music machine in a time outside of the 1970s. Elvis had 'left the building' a couple of decades earlier. But, Luigi's House of a Thousand Noodles was not your normal restaurant either. Just a few blocks from the state university, it was a frequent hangout for the campus full of students. The food was good. The prices were affordable. As long as you ate a meal and did not stay all night, Mr. Luigi would let the young people hang out in his booths for a few hours to study or socialize. You did, however, have to listen to Mr. Luigi's favorite music. Most of the crooners on his jukebox hung out with Sinatra and his Rat Pack, including the King of Rock and Roll.

Jared did not consider himself to be a romantic. He did not have the nerve to do some of the elaborate expressions of affection shown in movies. He did know, however, Lana had a firm grasp of his heart. Fear aside, an opportunity was standing before him. He needed to take advantage of it. That's why he rose, from the security of the corner booth with his two left feet, and walked toward the girl standing at the jukebox. He tapped Lana on the shoulder and extended his hand. There in the tiny little spot in front of the jukebox with a couple dozen sets of eyes watching, Lana and Jared had their first dance together to one of Presley's final hits, *Pledging My Love*. From then on, it would be their song.

Chapter Two

"WAKE UP, JARED KENNEDY. WE'VE got a lot to do today."

Jared rolled over in the king-size bed and put a pillow over his head as Lana poked her finger in his back. From under the pillow, he glimpsed a sliver of bright sunlight coming into the room. He had been awake for fifteen minutes but liked it when Lana woke him up on Saturday mornings. Saturdays normally meant lazy late breakfasts and coffee in bed as he channel-surfed to catch up on the world news and sports standings missed during a long work week. This Saturday had a different agenda. He grunted and pulled the pillow closer to his head.

"You are not going to sleep away this beautiful morning. There are houses out there waiting for us to find them. This might be the day we meet the home that is destined to be ours."

"Meet our house?" In one swift move, Jared flung the pillow away from his head, flipped over, and pulled Lana back into the bed as she turned to walk away. A scream escaped her mouth as her feet flew up into the air. It quickly turned into laughter as Jared began to roll her from side to side. In contrast to his jet black mane, Lana's strawberry blonde hair fell over his face as he pulled her toward him. Jared breathed in the scent of her shampoo. Despite being in her mid-twenties, Lana washed her hair with the same shampoo her mother used on her as a baby. It was one of the surprising habits of this complicated woman he loved so much. It was the freshest, happiest smell that Jared could imagine. He longed for the day when he would breathe in the smell from the soft hair of their child.

"For someone who has always touted the benefits of the mobility of renting, you sure do have the mortgage bug." Jared released her as she began to kick in retaliation to free herself from being slung around.

"That was before. Single girls have single agendas. This legal agreement that you and I entered into a few months ago has changed my perspective."

"Oh, darling, quit with all the romantic talk. It just makes me tremble for you to call our wedding a legal agreement." Jared jumped out of bed and put the back of his hand to his forehead like a woman faking a faint. "All this time, I thought you loved me because of my witty personality and six-pack abs. It's shocking to find out that it is all about my FICO score."

"Don't quit your day job, funny man. You do not have a future in comedy." Lana disappeared inside their walk-in closet as she kept talking. "There are three open houses today that I would like for us to hit. Two of them are for properties that our realtor says will probably go fast. You are the business one in this family; you should appreciate my research and planning."

"This family—I like the sound of that." Jared walked into the closet behind Lana and encircled her petite frame in an embrace. "When are we going to start working on that?"

"First, we need to get a house, and maybe have an anniversary under our belt before we start working on tax deductions." Lana turned around and gave Jared a quick kiss as she walked out of the closet.

"Mortgages and tax deductions. Who taught you the dirty talk? Besides, we've had plenty of anniversaries." Jared moved a couple of pieces of clothes before finding the polo shirt and jeans he wanted to wear.

"Anniversaries of first dates, twelfth dates, and proposals don't count. To be a big macho jock, you have a softie celebration side."

"I can't help that I have the heart of a romantic. If the truth was told, I think it was all of that romance that won you over." Jared began brushing his teeth.

"No." Lana pulled her hair into a ponytail. "It was something much more important than that." Sitting on the edge of their bed, Lana's expression turned serious. "It was that you got me. For the first time in my life, someone outside of my parents understood who I really was and accepted me for all of my idiosyncrasies. I know how complicated I can be. Creativity and obsessive compulsive tendencies can be a nerve-wracking combination. I could be myself with you. That's way more important than those rock solid abs of yours or the fact that every day is a celebration."

"That just saved me a lot of money and exercise."

Jared winked at Lana as he turned to go back into the bathroom. Hearing the phone ring, Lana left the room. As Jared began shaving, he thought about what she had just revealed. After meeting in the early days of college, their friendship had quickly turned to something deeper. After graduation, they had taken turns supporting each other as first Lana and then Jared pursued their advanced degrees for their chosen fields. Lana was an associate on the fast track to becoming a partner at a legal firm. Jared was an investment banker who specialized in portfolio management. They formed a little cocoon around themselves.

"Who was that on the phone?" Jared joined Lana in the kitchen a few minutes later.

"It was a new guy from work. His name is Trey."

"Haven't heard you mention him before. What did he want?"

"It was kind of strange. He asked if I could come by the office and get him the files for one of the cases we are working on."

"Well, you've done your share of weekend work. Guess he is doing the same."

"Trey isn't on the legal team. He works in accounting. He shouldn't be getting into our billable hours until the case is further along. Besides, that would be something that his supervisor would request from us."

"Maybe he is trying to impress management." Jared poured cereal into a bowl as Lana set a cup of coffee in front of him. He noticed a puzzled look lingering on her face. "There's something else that is bothering you about this, isn't there?"

"I don't know. Maybe I am reading too much into this. Every one of my encounters with him has been strange. Trey says that he went to college with us. I don't remember him at all."

"What's his last name?"

"Zachmann."

"Zachmann. I know someone by that name. It could be one of the brokerage clients though. No one from college is coming to mind. But, then again, we knew a lot of people just by their first names. Was he supposed to have been in our class?"

"No. He said he was about a year and a half behind us. Some story about that he had to take a semester off after his freshman year because of a health issue."

"What does he look like?"

"That's the thing. He has a dark beard and a moustache which he probably didn't have in college. That can change a man's entire look. Other than that, I would just describe him as average height and build. He's one of those people that nothing really stands out about."

"What did you tell him about work?"

"I told him that we weren't ready to close that particular case yet and that Nelson was the lead on it anyway."

"Did he accept that?" Jared pulled a banana from a bowl of fruit and began to peel it.

"I guess so. There was a little hesitation in his voice. Then, he asked me if I was having a good weekend." Lana rolled her eyes as she took her bowl to the sink.

"Did you tell him that you could be if he would stop bothering you?" Jared chuckled under his breath as he ate the banana. "Maybe he got behind on his work or something, and he's concerned since he is the new guy." Jared rose from the stool he was sitting on and took his bowl to the sink. "Get it out of your head. We've got to go look at mortgages." He ran his finger down the side of Lana's worried face.

"You mean houses." Lana's smile returned.

"You can call it what you want. This business guy sees a bottom line with lots of zeros for many years."

"CONGRATULATIONS TO LANA, who is becoming the youngest partner in the one hundred year history of Russberg, Sherman & Parsons."

Jared raised his glass of champagne as Lana's boss Paul Sherman spoke. A small group of friends and work associates had gathered to celebrate at her favorite restaurant. "I am so happy that I was smart enough to see the brilliance in this young woman even before she finished law school. Your five years at our firm have shown us what a dynamic future you have ahead of you. We look forward to having you on our team for many years to come."

Jared saw a few tears glistening in Lana's sparkling eyes. Normally shy regarding recognition, Jared noticed that tonight Lana seemed to truly be basking in her glory. He was happy to see her receiving recognition for all her hard work. It was his turn to toast his wife.

"Lana has worked tirelessly for this promotion. I've watched her spend countless nights and weekends devoted to fine tuning the cases she worked on. I am so proud of you, sweetheart."

A buzz of congratulations began as Jared sat down and watched their friends celebrate around her. The restaurant was busy for a Thursday evening with many small groups of people celebrating different events. From the corner of his eye, Jared caught a glimpse of someone standing along the wall in the corner of the restaurant. The man was dressed entirely in black. The color choice created a chameleon effect with the dark wall behind where he stood. Lana had risen and was standing next to Paul as she thanked him for his kind comments.

From the angle that Jared could see the man's profile gave the appearance of the man staring at Lana with a sly smile on his face. A suspicious feeling passed over Jared as he watched the man gaze at Lana. It reminded him of the gaze of a lion as it prepared to pounce on its prey. Jared's attention momentarily shifted as a waiter refilled his water glass. When Jared looked back up, the man was gone. He turned and looked around the restaurant, searching for the stranger. His attention was so fixed that he didn't realize someone was speaking to him.

"How is the house hunting going?" Deidre, Paul's wife, interrupted his searching. Jared had been watching the man so intently, he had not realized Lana had sat back down. "Paul told me that you are using the realtor we recommended."

"The realty firm is phenomenal." Lana caught Jared's eye as she spoke. "Their current selection of properties hasn't produced any possibilities for us yet."

"Translated that means that either the properties don't suit Lana or they are $100,000 more than we can afford."

"I understand. Perhaps the financial package that comes with becoming a partner will help."

"It will, Deidre. The firm has been very generous." Lana took another sip from her champagne glass. "Unfortunately, my college loan debt will be haunting me for a while yet. Excuse me for a moment." Lana got up and left the table.

"Lana put herself through law school. Her father was battling cancer during that time and there was little money left for her education. Becoming a lawyer was costly."

"It will pay off." Deidre's husband, Paul, spoke up. "Lana is the sharpest lawyer I have seen come along in my time with the firm. She will be given some high profile cases that will give her the opportunity to be financially rewarded for her hard work."

A few minutes passed and the entrees were served. Jared became concerned that Lana had not returned to the table. He excused himself and walked to the back of the restaurant toward the restrooms. As he passed the area where the man had been standing, Jared looked around but did not see him. As he turned toward the hallway where the bathrooms were, Lana came out the door.

"I was worried about you."

"I'm okay. I guess the excitement got to me a little. All the attention gave me a strange feeling, like I was being watched."

Jared started to reply but did not want to ruin Lana's evening.

"You are just excited. Shake it off. Let's go back and join our friends. Our meals have arrived. Bask in the glory, sweetheart, you have earned it."

The rest of the evening was full of laughter and good food. Jared caught himself looking toward the wall every so often. Despite what he had encouraged Lana to do, he could not shake off the feeling that there was something strange and familiar at the same time about the person he had seen.

"ARE YOU THINKING what I'm thinking?" Lana's voice was full of excitement.

"Lucky for you, I usually am." Jared pulled his wife into a hug as they stood in the foyer of the nineteenth house the realtor had shown them. "This is it?"

"This is it. I just love it. Even the Brady Bunch staircase." Lana kissed Jared on the cheek as she moved away from his embrace and stood at the steps of the staircase.

"That is so funny. It was my exact thought when I saw it. I could almost hear someone yelling 'Marcia.'"

"Maybe we should name our children after the Bradys." Lana turned and did a little dance as she twirled around the big empty area.

"Are we having that many? I'm going to enjoy that!"

"That was a joke." Lana's last twirl landed right in the middle of Jared's chest as she hugged him. "Seriously, this is the one. It's within our price range. It has most of the features we wanted. It has enough space for us to start a family. The backyard is huge."

"I really like the backyard and the garage."

"A triple garage! We have not seen any affordable houses with a triple garage."

"It's perfect. This is a good neighborhood, too. Morris Dillion from the accounting department lives one block behind this house, I think. I dropped him off after work one day when his car was in the shop. He talked about what a quiet area it was."

"Wonderful. I've never heard you mention him before. Does he have a family?"

"I really don't know." Jared paused to think for a moment. He knew very little about the man. He was surprised when Morris asked him for a ride. "That's the first and only time I ever actually had a conversation with him. He's a quiet sort. Those accounting guys usually are."

"Well, we will just have to get to know him better. He will be our neighbor." Lana walked toward the front door. "I just can't believe how wonderful this house is. Shag carpet and all. And, by the way, that carpet is going before we ever move the first box in."

Chapter Three

"**S**LOW DOWN, JARED. WHERE ARE you going in such a hurry?"

Jared's office chair was still spinning as he quickly walked by the adjacent cubicle. It was the end of a Wednesday workday, and his tall slender frame was almost skipping as it cruised past his co-worker.

"It's the twelfth anniversary of our first date." Jared gave Vince a huge grin as he stuck his head over the top of the cubicle wall. "It's got to be special."

"Man, you just make the rest of us look bad." Vince followed him down the hallway to the elevator. "I thought you two broke up for a while during college."

"Yep. I was an idiot. Thought I needed to play the field."

Jared pushed the down button. "Worst two months of my life."

"Two months doesn't seem that long."

The sound of a bell alerted that the elevator behind them was arriving. Jared quickly turned as the doors were sliding open.

"It's an eternity if you are with the wrong person." Both men got on the empty elevator. Jared pushed the button for the parking garage. "Or, in my case at the time, persons."

"You played the field then?" Vince slapped his friend on the back. "That's what college days are for."

"College days are for education and partying. Not for almost losing the girl of your dreams."

"Well, man, I wouldn't know. I haven't met mine yet."

"You will, Vince. Make sure you're paying attention when you do. Don't be a macho idiot. Don't let her get away."

The elevator stopped one floor before the garage. Jared forced a smile as a man from the accounting department got on.

"Hello, Morris."

"Hello." The man nodded and the doors closed.

"Where are you taking Lana for dinner?" Vince continued asking questions.

"Luigi's. It's a restaurant we practically lived in when we were in college."

Jared paused for a moment, and then turned his attention to the other man.

"I've been meaning to stop by your office, Morris." The man did not turn around as Jared spoke to him. "My wife and I have just moved into a house not too far from yours. It's on Plantation Street."

"Congratulations." The man still looked straight ahead.

"So, why are you celebrating a first date anniversary?" Vince resumed their conversation. "You're married now. You have a real anniversary coming up."

The elevator doors opened again. Jared got out quickly and turned back as his friend followed the man out.

"Because it's the day when infinity began."

"YOU HAVE GOT to be the most sentimental man ever put on God's green earth." Jared watched as Lana looked around the kitchen as she entered their new home from the garage. Every countertop had a vase of daisies on it—simple white petals with a yellow center, her favorite flower. "How did you possibly find so many?"

"I am now on a first name basis with every flower shop in town. The prettiest ones came from Petals. We might owe the owner our firstborn child."

Jared came up behind Lana and encircled her in an embrace. Despite the fact that it was the end of the day, he caught a whiff of her soft baby shampoo scent. It was the calming fragrance that he long ago began to associate with love. His love for this one girl.

"This must have cost a fortune. You know we need to save money. We have lots more things to do to this house." Lana furrowed her brow.

"Yes, daisies are known to be quite expensive, especially these plain Jane versions you love so much."

"Quit making fun. These daisies could have paid for trees for the yard."

"Okay. I will take them all back." Jared picked up the closest vase. "Maybe I could trade them on the street."

"You." Lana pushed her index finger into Jared's chest playfully. "It's a good thing that you pursued a banking career instead of one in comedy. We would starve to death." She put her arms around his neck. "You need to stick to trading stocks."

"Oh, yeah, that's what I do. I think trading daisies could be profitable. It could be a whole new market. They could be rated by petal count."

"Okay, wise guy. Where are you taking me for dinner since you spent all our money on the most beautiful flowers in the world?" Lana took a daisy out of a container on the kitchen counter and put the stem between her teeth. "I wonder if you can eat daisies."

"No eating daisies tonight. We are going to do the twelfth anniversary of our first date in style. We're going back to where it all began." Jared looked smug as he sat down on the brown leather stool on the other side of the breakfast nook.

"No. You don't mean."

"Yes, I most certainly do. We are a going to dine with a Mr. Luigi at his House of a Thousand Noodles." Jared altered his voice and gestures to mimic the Italian restaurant owner they both knew.

"You have got to be kidding." Lana shook her head as she walked toward the end of the couch where Jared's feet were. "That place is still open? Mr. Luigi couldn't possibly still be running it."

"It most certainly is. Mr. Luigi is eighty-five. His son runs it now."

"We are going to drive all the way back to the campus to eat—"

"The best spaghetti on the planet. It was your favorite meal our entire freshmen year. We ate there every week."

"I was eighteen and had only eaten spaghetti out of a can until then. Cooking wasn't Dad's best single parenting skill."

"Your Dad did just fine. You didn't starve. Mr. Luigi's spaghetti was wonderful. I'm sure it still is. In a couple of hours, we will find out."

"I REMEMBER YOU two. You went to the university a few years ago." A tall dark haired man seated them at a table in the back. "You still live around here? I've not seen you in the restaurant for a long time." The man gave Jared a questioning look.

"No. We moved away after graduation. We live about ninety minutes from here." Jared nodded to the man as he seated them at the booth he had requested. It was in the right hand corner where he and Lana always sat.

"What brings you to our humble establishment this evening?"

"It's the twelfth anniversary of our first date." Jared grinned. The man looked puzzled. "We had our first date here twelve years ago."

"Oh, I understand. A romantic evening to commemorate your first night of love. Italians understand love. We invented love, you know."

"You must be Mr. Luigi's son." Lana smiled as she took the menu he offered.

"Technically, I am Mr. Luigi too." The man winked at Lana. "But, I know you are referring to my old man—*the* Mr. Luigi. He just went home for the night. If you want to see him in the restaurant, you have to get here before six. He likes to get home these days in time to watch the news."

"He's still working? We thought he would be retired by now." Jared watched as a large party was seated at a table next to them.

"Retired? Absolutely not. My old man will work the lunch rush on the day of his funeral. He comes in at six each morning to make the sauce and the noodles. Everything is made fresh each day. He doesn't seem too interested in sharing the recipes. My daughter is beginning to join him in the mornings to try to learn his recipes. He is so secretive and thinks he will live forever."

"Romeo, you've got a phone call." The hostess yelled the message from across the restaurant.

"Excuse me. Enjoy your meal."

Jared and Lana burst out laughing once the man was out of earshot.

"Romeo? I don't remember him from when we used to come here." Lana laughed as she looked at the menu. "Oh, I remember these garlic rolls though. Yum."

"We were rather wrapped up in ourselves back then. We probably only remember Mr. Luigi because he talked to us so much."

"Like father, like son."

After the server took their orders, Lana and Jared began to relax.

"Have you left any rolls for me?" Jared reached into the basket as Lana gave him a smirk.

"We spent so many evenings here. I remember Mr. Luigi sitting down with us after the dinner rush was over. He would have a small, juice-size glass of wine and talk about growing up in Italy. His descriptions of the countryside were mesmerizing. We have to go there one day and experience it for ourselves." Lana looked around the restaurant. "It's obvious that they have made some upgrades to the place. It still feels the same though."

"It does. It feels like home. I think I felt as comfortable sitting at this booth as I did in my dorm room." Jared took a drink from the ice cold red plastic glass of water. "I can't even imagine how many plates of spaghetti I ate here. Mr. Luigi lost money when I would order the bottomless spaghetti. I was surprised to see it still on the menu."

"I don't know. You think you ate a lot. We would sit here and study as we ate. He probably made up for it off my tab."

"True. Your food consumption is significantly lower than mine. So many of our classmates were in here almost every day. All the parents ate here when they visited." Jared nodded as the server placed salads before them. "So before the spaghetti gets here and you see me revert to that teenage boy you used to know with my eating habits, tell me how things are going at work. We both have been putting in some long hours lately. That, coupled with the work we've been doing on the house, it seems like we haven't had any time to really talk."

"Work is crazy. Our caseload is exploding. Dexter just landed a huge corporate account with a regional chain of furniture stores that is about to become a nationwide chain. Get this? All of the furniture is made in the United

States. They are going to have stores in every state through regional franchises. We are doing all of the contracts and other agreements."

"I bet I know what company you are talking about." Jared smiled and shook his head. "We are leading parallel lives."

"What are you talking about?"

"We just learned about a new nationwide furniture chain that is going to go public with their stock. The corporate office is based here. They want our firm to help them with the public offering."

"Oh, my. We were destined to be together, weren't we? Even our jobs are married."

"We were destined to be together." Jared reached over and took Lana's hand. "It has nothing to do with our jobs." Jared released her hand as the server returned with their entrees. "What about that guy who said he went to school with us? I haven't heard you mention him anymore."

"Trey in accounting? Yeah, he must not have worked out too well. He was terminated a couple of weeks ago."

"Well, I hate to hear of anyone losing a job, but, it kind of made me uneasy with him calling you at home for no reason."

"I understand. I didn't even tell you the weirdest part." Lana began twirling spaghetti on her fork. "He showed up at the restaurant the night we had my promotion celebration."

Jared dropped his fork. It flipped off his plate and

landed on the floor. A young man bussing tables nearby saw it fall and quickly came over to pick it up, giving Jared a new set of silverware.

"He did what?"

"Trey showed up at the restaurant and watched us have dinner. Paul saw him while he was giving his speech. He said he was just staring at our table. Trey wasn't there having dinner or anything. He just came to watch. When Paul realized what was going on, he told him to leave. I think he had the manager escort him out. Just a few weeks later, Trey was gone. I guess it took human resources that long to gather up enough other documentation regarding his work and behavior."

For the second time, Jared withheld the information he knew from Lana. Tonight was another special celebration; it was not the right time to share what he had seen.

"I hope you are happy with my choice for tonight. This was a special place for us. We made a lot of plans here." Jared quickly changed the subject to prevent himself from dampening the mood.

"Yes, we did. It was like it was our place before we had one of our own. I'm so glad you brought me here this evening. This is a perfect night." Lana reached over and squeezed Jared's hand. "Soon, we will begin making some of those plans a reality."

"Onward to infinity." Jared gazed into Lana's eyes. He could see the future in her eyes. Within her gaze was where he really felt at home.

"I SHOULD NOT have eaten that second plate of spaghetti." Jared slid his seat back slightly as he waited for the traffic light to change. "It was like those meatballs were just taunting me. 'Just one more.' I can't remember the last time I felt so full. It's worse than Thanksgiving."

"I'm not sure I've seen you eat that much since the last time we ate there. Don't forget that basket of garlic rolls that you then slathered in more garlic butter."

"You ate more than salad yourself, young lady. It's a good thing that our wedding is long past now. You might have trouble fitting into your wedding dress." Jared turned off onto the two lane connector road that led back to their home in the city.

"That dress would still fit me just fine, mister. You vowed to love all of me, for better or worse. Garlic butter and spaghetti sauce oozing down my chin is part of the worse, right?" Lana began laughing.

"I will admit that your makeup probably could have used a touch-up."

"You love me anyway."

"Until infinity."

Jared could see Lana's hand automatically go to the necklace she was wearing. The necklace she had worn every day since he gave it to her twelve years ago.

"I wish I hadn't been so delusional back in college. We lost two months together because of my shortsighted outlook on life. When I think how close I probably came to losing you forever. I will never let that happen again."

"Stop beating yourself up about that, Jared. It is far, far in the past. In a way, I'm glad it happened. You sowed your wild oats and came back to me. Now, you're mine forever."

"Until infinity." Jared reached over and took her hand, briefly taking his eyes off the dark road ahead.

"Look out!"

Lana screamed and pointed. As Jared's attention went back to the road, he saw something dark coming toward the front of his Jeep Grand Cherokee. He cut the steering wheel to the left to try to avoid it. The vehicle jerked and began to spin, hitting something as it did. He heard Lana gasp. They spun and spun. Jared regained control and managed to stop the vehicle. Miraculously, the spinning vehicle had not flipped or gone off of the road. His heart was racing. He held his breath as he put the vehicle in park and turned to look at Lana. Her eyes were as big as saucers.

"Are you okay?" She nodded affirmatively. "I think I might have hit something." Jared reached for Lana. She was clutching her ribcage. "Are you sure you are okay? You are clutching your side." He looked around the interior of the Jeep. No glass was shattered. He wondered why the airbags had not released.

"Yes. I'm fine. Just shook up and frightened." Lana

looked into Jared's eyes. "I think the seatbelt dug into me while we were spinning. It all happened so quickly. Everything changed so fast."

"I'm going to get out and look for what we hit. Pray it wasn't a person."

"Be careful. It might have been an animal. It looked big." Lana reached out and put her hand on Jared's arm as he started to get out. "Don't go too far. I have a bad feeling about this. Maybe you should stay in the car, and we should call 911."

"We are okay. I'm not going to go any farther than around the Jeep. If it was an animal, it might have run off. We can alert the authorities once we know more about the situation."

Jared thought he saw a shadow fall on Lana's side of the Jeep as he looked back toward her. He closed his eyes and shook his head, thinking that his vision must be messed up from the spinning. He looked up and down the road to see if any vehicle lights could be seen heading toward them. Seeing none, he slowly opened the door and got out of the vehicle. He closed the door and carefully walked to the front of the Jeep. He heard Lana scream as he felt something hit him in the head from behind and felt his body collapse to the ground.

Jared had no idea how much time had passed. As he awoke, he felt himself being drug to the side of the road. A foot pushed on his side. Something broke inside him as he slid down an embankment. He couldn't see where he was rolling because of the darkness, but, he felt himself hit a large log. His mind flashed with the realization that there were steep cliffs on the right side of the road in the area. Even in his foggy state, Jared realized that the log stopped him from going down what could have been a very long drop. He needed to get back to Lana.

Despite the increasing pain, Jared began clawing his way back up. Was Lana still in the vehicle? He heard the Jeep start. Despite having what he was certain must be several broken ribs, he kept struggling to make it back up to the road. With each arm length he moved, the sound of the Jeep grew louder. He could see the taillights of the Jeep as he reached the point where the embankment met the road. As he tried to rise to his feet, Jared began to feel dizzy.

"LANA!"

Jared tried to steady himself. The Jeep's engine raced and the tires screeched as the vehicle began to pull away. Looking up he saw the moon cast its light on the window of the Jeep's hatch. Lana's terrified face and the palm of her right hand were all he saw as the Jeep sped away out of sight.

Chapter Four

"Mr. Kennedy, are you sure you don't remember seeing the person's face? Could it have been two people working together?"

With an icepack on the back of his head, Jared winced as a medic put a blanket on him and began to strap him onto the stretcher. A police officer hovered at the edge of the ambulance, trying to ask Jared questions.

"I don't know. It was dark. I don't think I saw two. I was dizzy from being hit on the head. I was trying to get back to the Jeep. Someone had come up behind me. It is all a blur." Jared's heart felt like it might explode with anger and worry. The throbbing of his head seemed to intensify, and every breath and movement shot piercing pain through his abdomen. "They are in my Jeep. It's a white Jeep. It should stick out, even at night. I gave some other officer a description of it and the license plate number. Why aren't you looking for it? Why are you talking to me when you could be looking for my wife?" Jared tried sitting up on the stretcher. Everything began to spin. Simultaneously, a sharp pain tore through his head while he cringed from the excruciating pain in his abdomen.

"You want to send someone with him?" The medic spoke to the police officer as he firmly took hold of Jared's shoulders and forced him to lie down. "We are about to transport him to St. Regis for further evaluation."

"No, I can't go to the hospital. I've got to look for Lana. He could have taken her anywhere. I've got to find her." Angry tears. Hot, angry tears flowed down his face.

"Mr. Kennedy, there are officers who have already been dispatched and are actively looking for your wife. It was fortunate that someone came along and saw you on the side of the road."

"I need to look for her. I've got to find her." Jared tried to rise again. This time the pain intensified and everything began to violently spin. The medic quickly put something underneath Jared's mouth as he threw up.

"Mr. Kennedy, you cannot help anyone until you get some medical care." The medic motioned for the officer to get out of the way and shut the ambulance doors. "We are taking you to the hospital. Your injuries are serious."

"Lana, Lana, I will find you." Jared lay back on the

stretcher as the ambulance began to move. His mind rewound the details of what had happened. His heart ached with fear.

"I'M CARY KENNEDY, his father, that's who I am, and you are going to get out of my way."

Jared opened his eyes and saw his father walking past a police officer and a nurse. His face filled with worry. The man did not seem to care that he had almost knocked down the officer and the nurse in his haste.

"Jared, what happened to you, son?" Mr. Kennedy reached for his son. Jared watched as his father looked at all of the machines and IVs that were hooked up to him. His father gripped the metal bed rail. The man's knuckles turned white, he was holding onto the rail so hard. "The police called me, but I didn't even wait to hear what they said. I just came rushing to the hospital. I got here as soon as I could. Were you in an accident?"

"We are still evaluating his condition, sir. It would be best if you left the room right now while we continue to treat him." Another nurse had followed Jared's father into the room.

"I will not leave the room until I know what is going on with my son."

"I'm okay, Dad. Let them do their work so that I can

get out of here and look for Lana." Jared raised his right hand and reached for his father. The man quickly grasped his son's hand.

"Look for Lana? I don't understand. Where is she? Wasn't she with you?" Mr. Kennedy turned toward the nurse. "Wasn't my son's wife in the accident, too? Where is she?"

Jared tightened his grip on his father's hand as his other hand reached to wipe the tears from his eyes.

"She's gone, Dad."

"Gone?" Mr. Kennedy returned his attention to his son. "You don't mean, she was—"

Jared shook his head. He started to speak, but he choked back tears instead.

"Sir, if I may?" Jared nodded as the police officer moved toward the bed. "Lana Kennedy was a passenger in the vehicle your son was driving. As I understand it, they thought the vehicle hit something or someone, causing Mr. Kennedy to momentarily lose control of the vehicle. After he regained control and stopped, he exited the vehicle to see what he hit. He was accosted from behind by an unidentified assailant and dragged away from the scene. He believes that he briefly lost consciousness. When he awoke, someone was driving off in his Jeep. Mrs. Kennedy was still in the vehicle. The perpetrator abducted her."

"They took Lana?" Jared's father looked at his son. Jared saw the look of horror that mirrored his own feelings as he shook his head. "We will find her, son. We will find her."

"Mr. Kennedy, I'm Detective Darren Oglesby. This is Detective Beth Rivers. We apologize for waking you, sir. We realize that you underwent surgery shortly after you arrived at the hospital and have only been out of recovery a few hours, but—"

"I'm Jared. Mr. Kennedy is that gray haired guy guarding me from that chair over there." Jared pointed to his father. His father's head was bobbing as he dozed in the dark corner. "I don't care about sleep. I don't care about my injuries. I want to get out of this bed and look for Lana. I want everyone looking for Lana."

Jared's head was still pounding despite the doses of pain medication he had been given. His whole body felt like one big pain. It was nothing compared to the fear that was beginning to consume him.

"I can assure you, sir, we are doing everything in our power to find your wife. We have enlisted state and federal law enforcement assistance. A team with the FBI that specializes in abductions is on their way."

"Abduction." Jared took a deep breath that caused him to gasp in pain from his broken ribs and other injuries. "That's the kind of word you hear on the news. You don't expect it to be applied to your own life."

"No, sir. You do not."

Detective Rivers approached Jared's hospital bed. The female agent appeared to be in her early thirties. Jet black hair was cut in a blunt shoulder length style. Minimal makeup and even less jewelry accompanied her standard navy blue detective suit. Jared was struck by the thought that she looked like she had just walked off an episode of *Law & Order*. Her sidekick appeared to be in his late forties with the beginnings of a receding hairline and a belly that hung over his belt. They were the stereotypical detective team. He closed his eyes and shook his head.

"Are you okay? Should I get the nurse?" Detective Oglesby spoke to him from the opposite side of the bed. The officer had a panicked look on his face.

"No, I am not okay, detective. But, this whole hospital of medical personnel cannot fix me." Jared winced as he raised his voice. "I am looking at the two of you and am realizing that my life is now an episode of a crime drama. Somehow, I don't think you are going to be able to solve this in the one-hour time slot."

"That's a correct deduction, sir." Detective Rivers resumed talking. "We are here though to gather as much information from you as possible to help us find Lana."

Detective Rivers pulled up a chair next to Jared's bed and Detective Oglesby followed on the other side.

"Sir. What were you and Lana doing last night?"

"We went and had dinner over in Taylorsville."

"That's quite a distance away to have dinner on a Wednesday night. Was it a special occasion?"

"Yes. It was the twelfth anniversary of our first date."

Detective Rivers looked up from her notepad and smiled. The other detective looked a little confused.

"Was this dinner your idea or Lana's?"

"It was mine. I was the one who liked to celebrate our first date. I think of that night as when my life first started."

"Sounds like a special relationship."

"Why Taylorsville?" Detective Oglesby interjected.

"We went to college at the university there. That's where we met. We had our first date at an Italian restaurant there."

"House of a Thousand Noodles, I bet." Detective Rivers laughed. "Is Mr. Luigi still there?"

"Yes, during the day. We talked to his son last night." As Jared heard his own words, his mind could not process that it had just been the night before. Hours seemed like days. The rush of emotion caused a lump in his throat.

"I worked there one summer. That family is something else. Mr. Luigi wouldn't even tell Romeo the sauce recipe."

"Apparently that is still the case, according to Romeo." Jared coughed to try and stop himself from crying. Detective Rivers picked up the cup of water that was next to his bed. She aimed the straw at his mouth and allowed him to get a sip. "Thank you. Romeo has his daughter working with her grandfather to try and learn how to make it. I can't imagine how old Mr. Luigi must be now."

"So, what time did you leave the restaurant?" Detective Oglesby cleared his throat as he brought the conversation back to its topic.

"It was about a quarter to nine."

"The bypass doesn't have too much traffic that time of night. Why did you take the back roads instead?"

"Habit. It's the route I always took when I was in college. I grew up here. The bypass wasn't built until after I graduated."

"Where did Lana grow up?" Detective Rivers rejoined the conversation. "Is she from nearby as well?"

"No. Lana grew up in several places. Her father was career military. By the time Lana was in college, her father had retired and they were living outside of Baltimore."

"I believe our information states that her parents are both deceased. Is that correct?" Detective Oglesby flipped through a few papers in a file as he asked his question.

"Yes. Lana's mother died in a car accident when Lana was in elementary school. Her father passed away a couple of years ago of cancer."

"No siblings?"

"No. She has a couple of aunts and uncles and a few cousins. But, she really isn't close to any of them. Christmas cards, maybe an occasional phone call."

"So, it's not likely that she might have gone to visit one of them?" Detective Oglesby did not look up as he asked his question. "If she was going to go visit someone, who do you think that would be?"

"Are you out of your mind?" Jared tried to sit up in the hospital bed. His whole body shook with pain. "Lana was taken. Taken against her will. She's not gone off on a weekend getaway or a family reunion. We were attacked."

"Calm down, Mr. Kennedy." Detective Rivers stood up and moved closer to Jared. Several lights were flashing and alarms were sounding on the machines that he was hooked up to. "We understand what you have told us."

Jared watched as Detective Rivers gave Detective Oglesby a stern look and shook her head. His yelling had caused his father to awaken as a nurse came rushing into the room.

"Mr. Kennedy, why are you sitting up in bed?" The nurse was an older woman. She firmly pushed Jared back down. As she checked several of the lines into the machines, she punched several buttons making the alarms stop. "Am I going to have to ask you two to leave?"

"No, ma'am. He just got a little agitated about one of our questions." Detective Oglesby replied as his eyes darted to Jared. "He misunderstood my intent."

"I misunderstood nothing. I can see where this is going. I'm going to be treated like a criminal while the real criminal does God-knows-what to Lana."

"You can't keep me here against my will." Jared's voice grew louder as the conversation with the doctor continued.

"No one seems to understand me. I have got to get out of this place and find my wife."

Almost a week had passed since Lana had been abducted. Jared had first undergone surgery to make sure the internal bleeding, caused by his multiple broken ribs, was repaired. Then, there were several scans of his head done to make sure that the blow he received did not result in any bleeding on the brain. Further complications in the days after led to a second surgery as fluid had entered his lungs. Strong medications for pain gave him an altered sense of reality.

Despite the seriousness of his injuries and the pain he was in, with each passing hour that he spent in the hospital, Jared's anxiety grew. Updates from the police, as well as almost constant reports on the television news, told him that everything was being done to search for her. The outpouring of volunteers had gone from dozens to hundreds to thousands in a matter of a few short days. Every day, Jared's fear grew—the fear that he would never see Lana again.

"Son, the police are out there looking for Lana. There are thousands of volunteers looking as well. It's been amazing the people who have come out to help. I've received phone calls from the parents of kids you went to school with and from old work friends of mine I haven't seen in years. One community three counties away organized and sent over two hundred people as well as a truckload of food for the volunteers."

Jared's father stood by the bed. He knew that his father was trying to encourage him. But he thought he saw the man aging before his eyes. No one had to tell him that this nightmare might not have a happy ending. Jared wondered what his own reflection would reveal.

"Listen to the doctor. You will not be any good to Lana until you have healed from this."

"I will never heal from this."

The words came out easily without stumbling or emotion. The reality of the pure truth in them hit Jared between the eyes. Lana's physical life might be over. His physical life might continue. It would never be better. There was no light at the end of the tunnel for him. There was no light in his life without Lana

"Mr. Kennedy, you have made tremendous progress in the last forty-eight hours. Don't ignore the fact that you had life-threatening injuries. If you had not been able to climb back up that embankment, the internal bleeding would have killed you. You must rest. I understand the situation and your anxiousness to be released."

"Understand? Do you, doctor? Has anyone you loved ever been taken away before your very eyes?" Jared heard the bitterness in his words. It was like he was hearing someone else's voice. It was like hearing a foreign language. One he had been forced to learn.

"If you continue to improve, I will release you tomorrow." The doctor turned and began to walk out of the room. He stopped at the door and turned back around. "There is a whole community of people out there, Jared, who want to help you. Your friends, your coworkers, your neighbors, and even strangers like me. You are living our biggest fear. We feel helpless. Let us help you in the few ways that we can. I can only treat your injuries, but, as a community, we will never stop looking for Lana."

Jared took a deep breath as the door closed behind the doctor. His father walked to the window and looked outside.

"All the national news crews are here, Jared. Lana's face is probably on every news station in the country by now. Someone will see and recognize her. Someone will call in a tip that will help the authorities find her."

Jared had forgotten that Detective Rivers was in the room. She had arrived a few moments before the doctor had. This time, she was without her sidekick.

"I interviewed Romeo Luigi yesterday." Her voice was calm. "He said that he remembered seeing you two that night."

"You two. Such a simple statement. We may never be that again."

"I'm sorry, Jared. That was thoughtless of me." Detective Rivers' voice sounded less calm. She began to pace around the bed. "Romeo Luigi contacted us after he learned of Lana's disappearance."

"It must have freaked him out that he had just seen us in his restaurant after all of those years."

"More than that, he thought he might have some information that could help."

Jared used the bed remote to adjust himself in an upright position. It was still painful to move, but not nearly as much as it had been. The newspaper his father was reading fell to the floor.

"I don't understand. What type of information?"

"Romeo Luigi said that he remembered seating someone right after you came in and that the same person left just minutes before you did. He said that it was a man. Romeo said that there was something about the man that just didn't seem right. When he heard the news about the abduction, he remembered the encounter."

"What was strange about his behavior?" Jared's father beat him to the question.

"He entered the restaurant shortly after you and Lana arrived. For a while, the man did not order any food. When he finally ordered, the man never touched it after it was served. Even Romeo noticed that the man was not eating and asked him if something was wrong. The man told him that he wasn't hungry."

"I would say sitting in a restaurant and not eating the food you ordered is strange behavior." Jared's father sat back down in his chair.

"So, this might not have been some random act. Whoever took Lana might have planned it?" Jared could feel his heart begin to race.

"It's possible. Or, this man could not have been involved and was exhibiting some strange behavior."

"Are there security cameras at the restaurant?"

"Yes, there are. We have scanned them. All we could see was a blur when the man entered."

"Even at the cash register? Surely, they have a camera there."

"They do. But the man paid his server at the table. He paid in cash, so no credit card receipt."

"Why did you tell me this then?" Jared leaned back down on the pillows. Exhaustion showed on his face.

"To give you hope."

"Hope? How is hearing about a dead end piece of information going to do that?"

"Lots of leads will come. Perhaps one of them will give us crucial information to help find her."

"If the man at the restaurant followed us there and is the one who took Lana, what does that mean?" Jared paused. He thought about possible scenarios. "Does that mean that he might keep her—"

Jared watched Detective Rivers' expression. He knew he needed to hear her response to make sense of the situation, a dread formed in him unlike any he knew before.

"There's no simple answer to that question, Jared. As much as the criminal mind has been examined, each one is still as different as the individual. Profilers can make general statements that could predict what might occur, but it is really a gamble."

"You're evading the question. What do you think?"

"If someone followed you and Lana to that restaurant, I think it was more than just a random act. He knew something about you. Who goes out to dinner on a Wednesday night over an hour away from their home? Only someone with a special occasion to celebrate."

"Do you think we might know this person?"

"Perhaps, or it could be someone who has spent a great deal of time studying your habits."

"Lana's habits?"

"Yes, but how those habits interact with both of your lives."

Jared took a deep breath and shifted his gaze to the window. The bright sun made the blue sky pop with color. It should have been a normal day for Lana and him. Going to work. Running errands. Planning dinner. Doing the things that people must do to keep their lives moving forward. Moving forward now seemed like a foreign concept. His mind drifted back to the restaurant as the officer spoke.

"Jared, you said that the dinner was to celebrate your first date. Who would know that? Would that have been something that Lana would have talked about?"

"I don't think so. I was the one who made a big deal out of it. I was the more sentimental of the two of us. She joked that her childhood of skipping around the world as a military brat without a mother caused her not to develop the sentimental gene. I can't imagine that she would talk about our first date to her co-workers, if that is what you mean. Lana is very private, guarded."

"I need a list of her friends with contact info, if you have it."

Jared nodded and reached for a small notepad. One of the officers that had interviewed him early on had given it to him to use if he remembered anything while the police were not around.

"Jared, it is time for us to get you up for a shower." A male nurse came into the room.

"I'll come back later." Detective Rivers headed for the door.

"You didn't answer my question."

Detective Rivers stopped at the door. Jared watched her shoulders rise and fall as she took a deep breath.

"If this was a planned abduction of Lana specifically, he may keep her alive."

"Because—"

The detective turned and looked Jared in the eyes.

"Because he wanted what you have."

ALL NIGHT LONG Jared's dreams were full of scenes of Lana reaching out to him. No matter how hard he tried, Jared could not reach her. Despite the fact that he had been given pain meds to help him sleep, he was wide awake in the darkness of four o'clock.

Perhaps, it was the shallowness of the hour or the sleep deprived state of his mind that made the crazy thoughts start running through his brain like a treadmill that would never stop. He tried to remember all of the people that he and Lana had been around in the last few weeks and months. Jared tried to recall anyone who seemed to let their eyes stay on her a little too long or who seemed too interested in the details of their lives.

The only person Jared could think of was the person he and Lana had talked about over dinner at the restaurant. He had immediately told police officers about Trey from Lana's firm and how peculiar his behavior had been on two separate occasions that Jared knew about. Jared was furious with himself for not telling Lana what he had seen on the night of her promotion celebration. Detective Rivers had told him that Trey Zachmann had died of an overdose a few weeks before the abduction. It haunted him, just the same.

The exercise of remembering during those wee hours of the night only proved what he already knew. As a couple, he and Lana were quite reclusive. It had been just the two of them for so many years, it was a rare occasion for them to be part of four or six or a dozen. Someone would have had to be watching closely from afar to know what Jared had planned for that Wednesday evening. It had to be someone who was invisible in his life.

Chapter Five

"I DON'T THINK I NEED A police escort."

Jared carefully sat down in a wheelchair as he prepared to leave his hospital room. Over a week had passed since Lana was taken.

"We need to talk to you, Jared."

"What's happened?" Jared searched the face of Detective Oglesby for some indication of what the man was going to say. He could see from the open door that Detective Rivers was talking to his father. A stern look crossed the elder Kennedy's face. "You've found her?" A mixture of hope and fear was in his tone.

"Let's get you to the vehicle downstairs. Media is everywhere. We are going to take you out through the service corridor."

A nurse began to wheel Jared out the door. Making brief eye contact with his father told him nothing. Detective Rivers had walked ahead toward the elevator before Jared crossed the threshold from his room. Stoic silence alternated with the dings of the elevator as it made its way into the basement.

A wave of fear passed over him as he saw the arrow pointing to the morgue as they exited the elevator. Instinctively, he reached for his father who was standing next to him.

"No, we are not going—"

Jared felt the soft hand of Detective Rivers on his opposite shoulder as she whispered in his ear.

"It is okay, Jared. We are just exiting this way. We are not stopping anywhere."

Jared let out the breath that he had not realized he had been holding. His father's hand gripped his own as Mr. Kennedy must have realized what his son was thinking.

The wheelchair zipped down a narrow hallway and automatic double doors flew open letting in the light of a bright midday sun. The brightness glared on the back window of the SUV that was waiting. Jared momentarily flashed back to the glint of the moon on his own vehicle and the image of Lana's palm on the window. Jared stood up before the wheelchair had stopped, lurching forward and almost falling as he heard his own piercing voice.

"LANA!!!"

The male nurse and Detective Oglesby moved in stealth speed as they grabbed hold of Jared and quickly steered him to the open rear door of the passenger side of the vehicle. Detective Rivers hopped into the front seat on the passenger's side while Jared's father slid in next to him on the driver's side. Jared heard the doors slam as he saw reporters and cameramen rush the front of the vehicle as it began to drive away.

"Sorry that we had to manhandle you, Jared. But it is probably best that you have a planned media experience." Detective Oglesby spoke from the driver's seat of the SUV.

"What happened to you, Jared? What did you see?" Sitting in front of Jared, Detective Rivers turned her body to be able to look him straight in the eyes.

"I had a flashback of that night. I saw this vehicle and it just took me back to seeing my Jeep driving away with Lana in the back."

"Did it make you remember anything else? Relax your mind and think for a moment. Focus on it."

"Do you think this is really the time? My son has just left the hospital."

"He's just had a flashback, Mr. Kennedy. His memory is fresh."

"I remembered Lana. It just hit me. I saw her hand."

"In the back window? Have you told us that before? Lana wasn't in the front seat?"

"No. She was in the back. I saw her hand on the glass, like she was reaching for me. It's my last—"

Jared lurched forward in the backseat as the vehicle suddenly stopped. The Detective Oglesby blew the horn and swore under his breath. Jared looked up and saw a cameraman standing in the middle of the road. A police officer pulled him away and the SUV turned onto the street.

"Why are there so many media here to watch me leave the hospital?"

"It's a media frenzy." Detective Oglesby put on his seatbelt. "You've seen it with other cases. The media has branded this as the Anniversary Abduction. You might as well start preparing to see your face a lot on television and the internet. Some of these more aggressive reporters probably already know more about you than you remember."

"My face? It's Lana's face that should be out there."

"It is, Jared. The media can actually be quite helpful." Detective Rivers pulled out her cell phone and showed Jared a website that had already been set up to solicit information. "The dark side of it is that they also have to keep telling a little something new to keep people watching. You will be shown as everything from the distraught husband to an accomplice in the crime."

"Accomplice? Is that what you think?" Jared's head began to throb.

"We had to investigate you, of course. We have to eliminate all possibilities. It didn't take us long to realize that there were no holes in your story. You were too seriously injured. There were traces of your blood found all the way down that bank. If it hadn't been for you hitting a log, I'm not sure how long it would have taken for you to be found. The evidence told us that you did not do this to yourself."

"It's a shame that his word was not good enough. That the grief and anguish that was pouring out of him was not sufficient." There was disgust in Mr. Kennedy's voice. "I dare you to find anyone who has an ill word about my son."

"Oh, Dad, I'm sure there is someone." Jared reached over and squeezed his father's arm. "Obviously, there was someone who wanted me gone. My mind just can't figure out who it is."

"We want you to keep thinking and remembering. There might be a sliver of something that will help the investigation. Just realize that it might also not be there." Detective Rivers paused as her phone beeped. She checked it and returned it to her pocket. "You might not have known this person at all, even casually. Coveting is not a new concept. It is not unusual to want something you can't have. It starts in childhood. Most people learn to either control that desire or to pursue it in a meaningful way, such as working hard to earn money to buy that big house. A few people let such a desire fester and grow and try a shortcut to the fulfillment of it."

"Do you think my son is in any further danger?" Mr. Kennedy's question came as they were turning the corner onto the block where Jared and Lana lived. "Maybe he should stay with me for a while."

"I think I will be fine at home." Home. Would their house still be a home without Lana?

"Jared, you need to understand before we get there that the police have searched it." Detective Oglesby spoke as he slowed down for a stop sign. "There may be a few things out of place."

JARED FINALLY CONVINCED his father that it was okay to leave him alone for a little while. To keep his father busy and feeling useful and in order to have a few quiet moments by himself, Jared asked him to go get a few groceries and some dinner for them. While he was gone, Jared hobbled around the house looking at what the police had done in their search.

"A few things out of place." Drawers were open. Closets looked like items had been moved around. The vases of dead daisies only added to the sad condition. "Lana would be ticked."

As Jared heard the words come out of his mouth, he sunk to the floor at the breakfast nook in the kitchen. The crying began. By the time his father returned, Jared's eyes were swollen. The effort of sobbing only inflamed the pain of his broken ribs and other injuries.

"Jared, did something happen? What's wrong, son?"

"She's gone, Dad. I know that I should hold on to every shred of hope that I can, but my gut tells me that this is never going to get better. Somebody wanted my Lana. Somebody saw how perfect my life was and wanted it for himself. May God help me, but I don't blame him. I was the luckiest man in the world."

"And you knew it, son. You loved her every minute of every day. She knew that." Jared's father got down on the floor next to him. "You can't give up. Not as long as she's out there and you don't know where. If the worst happens and they find a body, you can bury her. Until then, you've got to keep looking. You married her; you promised her forever."

"I promised infinity."

"I know that symbol has a special meaning between the two of you." Mr. Kennedy pulled his son into an embrace. "You had already given her that necklace by the time I met her. I remember you calling me and asking for some extra money to buy something for a girl. I wondered how many times I would hear you say that to me. I soon learned that she just wasn't a girl, she was *the* girl. I do not believe that I ever saw her without that pendant around her neck."

"It was special to us. Actually, that symbol was special to her before I even met her. I think Lana had imagined what we would have even before we met."

"Did she ever tell you why it was special to her?"

"She talked about it once when I was brave enough to

ask about her mother." Jared let his mind wander to the long ago conversation.

"You've not talked much about your mother. I understand it can be hard. I lost mine to cancer a few years ago."

Jared and Lana sat in her dorm room. Nearing the end of their freshman year, they were using most of their free time to study for the dreaded final exams. Yet their relationship had already reached a point where every waking hour possible was spent together.

"It's sad to say, but my time with her almost seems like another life. It seems so far away that I often wonder if my memories are my own or stories that others have told me about her." Lana closed her biology book and clutched it to her chest. "I remember her making me oatmeal and dropping cinnamon raisins in it, one by one."

"Cinnamon raisins?" Jared scrunched his nose and furrowed his brow. "What are they?"

"Mom used to buy these little boxes of cinnamon raisins and put them in my lunch box. Some mornings, she would make oatmeal for breakfast. I remember that she would set the steaming bowl in front of me. I can still see her with one of those little boxes, taking each raisin out individually and dropping it into the oatmeal. When it got down to the bottom of the little box, she would put a raisin in my mouth and eat the last one herself."

Jared watched Lana's face as she was lost in memory. Her eyes were staring straight ahead, but they were obviously not seeing what was actually in front of her. The view she was gazing on was a different time and place.

"What happened to her?"

"She was in a car accident. We lived on the military base. I was in school when it happened. Dad was away on assignment. I remember the commanding officer of the base and his wife coming to the school to get me. He was very tall."

Jared watched as Lana got off her bed and went over to her desk. She took a small framed photograph from the back of one of the shelves. He had never noticed it being there. Lana paused to look at the photo for a moment before she handed it to him.

A little girl with pigtails stood in front of a beautiful young woman. Jared could see Lana in the little girl and in the woman.

"Mom is the reason I love infinity symbols. She had a small tattoo of one on her ankle. I used to sit in the floor next to her leg and trace it over and over with my finger. She promised me that when I turned eighteen, she would let me get one just like it, if I still wanted to."

"I've never noticed that you have a tattoo."

"She wasn't here to take me to get one."

Jared closed his eyes as he realized what he had said.

"I'm sorry, Lana. That was a stupid thing for me to say."

"It wasn't stupid. It was a logical thought. I guess I could have gone and got one. My heart just wasn't in it anymore. I didn't want to do it without her." Lana sighed as she took the photo from Jared and returned it to the spot on her desk. "But it didn't change my love for the symbol. To me, it represents love. I know that even though she is physically gone, her love is still with me. Nothing can change that. Pure love is limitless. It is infinity in its truest sense. What else would forever be for than pure and boundless love?"

Lana went back to her biology book. Although Jared appeared to do the same, his mind was still focused on what Lana had said. Pure and boundless love—he was certain that was what he felt in his heart for Lana. Somehow, his mind could not imagine such a feeling for anyone else.

"What was Lana's mother's name, son?" Jared and his father were still sitting on the floor when he finished telling his memory. "I don't believe I ever remember Conrad speaking of her."

"From what Lana told me later, I don't believe that Conrad ever forgave himself for being away when Lana's mother had the accident. You understand what a burden it is to feel helpless when the woman you love dies."

"I do, son. But, like in my case, you cannot carry that burden forever. Conrad had a job to do."

"Her name was Victoria. I think Lana's father called her Tori."

Jared grew silent as he thought about how both he and Lana had lost their mothers before adulthood. He knew that despite his words, his father still wondered what he could have done to save his own wife. Jared wondered if he was destined to carry a similar burden.

The phone rang, and Jared's father slowly rose to answer it.

"There's a reason why old men don't sit in the floor." Mr. Kennedy chuckled softly as he struggled to rise. "Hello." He looked down at his son as he listened to the person on the other end. "Yes, he is right here, Detective Rivers." Mr. Kennedy handed him the phone, and then walked back into the kitchen.

"Hello." Jared felt his heart rate begin to rise as he waited for Detective Rivers to speak.

"Jared, this is Beth Rivers. I hope you have been getting some rest."

"Rest. I guess you could call it that. Have you found out something?"

"No, there's nothing new regarding the case."

"Why are you calling?" Jared knew it was going to get harder to conceal his frustration with no progress in finding Lana.

"We would like for you to go on television tomorrow and make a plea to the public to help find Lana."

"Okay. What time? Where do I need to be?"

"Ten o'clock tomorrow morning. We will do it at the police station. Do you want us to come and get you?"

"No, I can get there on my own."

"Please get here by around nine. We have a prepared statement for you."

"A prepared statement. That sounds nice and formal. Don't you think that my speaking from the heart would be better?"

"These things are more effective when the communication is planned."

"I see." Jared hung up the phone.

"What do they want you to do, Jared?"

"They want to hold a press conference tomorrow morning. They want me to make a prepared statement to the public. How can they possibly know what I need to say?"

"Well, I'm sure they know what they are doing."

"Do they? How can you be sure? How can we be sure of anything when everything that is right is now wrong?"

Chapter Six

"**M**Y NAME IS JARED KENNEDY. I need your help." Jared looked straight into the camera. "On the night of October 16, after celebrating the anniversary of our first date, my wife, Lana Bouvier Kennedy, and I were brutally attacked on our way home. Lana was abducted, and I was left for dead on the side of the road. For the last week, I have been in the hospital recovering from the physical injuries inflicted by the person or persons who took my wife. I would like to have been looking for her." Jared swallowed hard as a lump formed in his throat.

"The photo on the screen is my beautiful Lana. We met when I was eighteen years old. I have loved her every day since that moment. We were married just a few months ago. Lana is a brilliant lawyer who just became a partner at the firm where she works. Maybe someone out there has seen her in the past few days. Maybe someone knows who took her and wants to help us bring her home. Maybe someone understands that Lana is my entire world, and I will do anything to have her back."

He had strayed off the script that Detective Rivers had written. Jared could see a look of displeasure cross her face. Yet, she nodded for him to continue.

"I am asking for your help. The only way that I will ever be reunited with the love of my life is if someone out there helps us find her. If you see anything or know anything that might help the police with their investigation, please contact the number on the screen or go to the website and send a message. I beg you." Jared swallowed the lump in his throat. "Lana, if you can hear this, please know that I love you more than life itself. I wish that this person would have taken both of us. I would give anything to be with you. I will never stop looking, so don't you give up. It will always be until infinity." Jared looked down at his trembling hands. The movement made the papers shake and hit the microphone. He released the papers and balled his hands into fists. "Until infinity, my darling. This is my pledge. Somehow, I will find you."

The segment was televised live from a small room in the police headquarters. As soon as Jared was finished speaking, one of the FBI agents returned to the microphone and finished talking about the investigation. As Jared listened to him giving out details that he knew all too well, he glanced around the room at the faces of the journalists. Their solemn expressions spoke volumes. He imagined that these would be faces he would begin to recognize as the days passed. Jared forced his attention to return to what the officer was saying as he heard the man describe characteristics to look for if someone suspected an individual they knew.

"Keep in mind. This person could be anyone. As the days go forward and we gather more details, we may be able to offer more information. Until then, I am going to share some general characteristics. While a nationwide manhunt is underway, it is equally important for local and regional residents to be especially on alert. We do not believe this was a random act. Several pieces of evidence led us to draw the conclusion that this was a planned and premediated kidnapping of Lana Kennedy specifically. We believe that the perpetrator has probably stalked the Kennedys for quite some time."

Jared watched as a reporter raised her hand.

"Please hold your questions until I have finished." The officer nodded at the reporter. "Immediately following the kidnapping, the person may have been absent from work. This might have been an unplanned absence or a no-show. Upon returning, he may have offered some plausible, but shallow, excuse such as a sudden illness, car trouble, or a death in the family. The person might also have missed planned appointments such as a medical visit or even a scheduled appointment with a probation officer. You might notice that the person may have an unusual interest in the media coverage of this case, or, conversely, may suddenly turn the coverage off each time it appears. A key sign would be an extreme reaction one way or another."

Another officer approached from behind and whispered in the speaker's ear. Jared cast hopeful eyes from him to Detective Rivers. She nodded her head negatively.

"The perpetrator may increase consumption of alcohol or drugs. Changes to appearance such as altering hair color or growing a moustache or beard, are also common signs. Additionally, the person may try to modify the appearance of a vehicle or trade vehicles. Leaving town suddenly with little or no explanation is also a red flag." The officer took a drink of water from a bottle under the podium. "Let me be very clear. It is very likely that someone who is watching this right now knows the individual who committed this crime. Due to the nature and severity of injuries to Mr. Kennedy, we believe that this abduction was committed by at least one male. But, there could also have been an accomplice to help carry out the act of abduction. This person is someone's coworker, neighbor, casual acquaintance, or friend. He is a member of someone's family. In order to effectively carry out this crime, he has interacted with many people in this community and regional area. Keep an open mind as you think about this situation. Do not fear that you will cause problems for innocent people by contacting the police. An innocent person has nothing to fear. An innocent person will be quickly cleared. Someone knows this person. Someone can help us find Lana Kennedy."

The officer took a few brief questions, and then concluded the press conference. Reporters were yelling questions at Jared, but he was whisked out of the room before he could answer.

"Why didn't we stay in there and answer more questions? Those people can help us."

"We have given them all of the information they need to do their job."

"But something else I might say could help." Jared could not remember the name of the officer who was the spokesperson. He seemed to be a superior to Detectives Rivers and Oglesby. "I want to talk to them."

"Your emotions are raw. You deviated off of the prepared statement. The purpose of this was for you to appeal to the public for their help. I don't want you to start getting angry and do something like threaten the kidnapper."

"Like that person doesn't know I am angry? What difference does it make?"

"Jared, I realize this is beyond anything you ever dreamed you would be experiencing. We understand that you are mentally and physically in anguish. But, with all due respect, you are not thinking clearly." Jared started to speak, but the man held up his hand. "The mental state of someone who can commit an act as heinous and calculated as kidnapping is complicated. A huge part of his psyche is that he wants something that someone else has. This guy doesn't admire you and want to emulate you, he hates you. He wants to see you angry. He will feed on it."

"I still don't understand why that matters. He was successful in his plan. He's got Lana."

"What I am trying to tell you is that is only part of it. He wants to feel superior to you. We will only give him limited access to see you. That's why we did not want you to deviate from the script. If he doesn't know how you are, he may slip up to try to find out."

"You mean he may try to contact Jared?" Mr. Kennedy spoke from the corner of the room. "Is my son in danger? Why hasn't he had police protection?"

"He has police protection, sir. You both have from the very beginning. There are several officers stationed around Jared's home. When you went out yesterday to the store, an officer followed you, and others remain stationed around the perimeter of the house."

"How in the world—? I never saw anyone." Mr. Kennedy sat down and put his head in his hands.

"That's the whole point, Mr. Kennedy. Our officers need to appear invisible. If someone approaches Jared in any way, we will be there. We will be able to follow that person back to wherever he is holding Lana."

"You can't do that forever." Jared sat down in a chair

near the wall. His body was telling him that it was time for another dose of the pain meds.

"We hope we won't have to." Detective Rivers sat down beside him. "If this guy has planned this abduction carefully, he has studied your life pattern. He may have gotten close enough to know your emotional reactions to situations. It probably started with him envying the relationship between you and Lana. It may have progressed to him even trying to get to know you."

"You mean this guy might have tried to become our friend?"

"It may be a long shot theory. Yet, it could be quite possible. You have already told me that you two did not socialize a lot. That's probably, in part, due to both of you having busy work schedules and the fact that you were also caught up in planning your wedding, and then moving into a new home. Maybe you blew this guy off. Maybe you didn't even realize he was being friendly. This is all speculation. But if even one of these fragments of theory is close to the truth, this guy wants to know what your reaction is. He took what you had. Part of his joy is to see you suffer."

"DAD, I CAN'T HELP but think about what the officer said earlier. This person might be someone that Lana and I knew or at least had met. My mind has been running in circles thinking about people. You know, you can easily make a list of people you consider your friends, but acquaintances, that's a whole other story. There's hundreds of people that you casually know and come in contact with repetitively. You never think about how many people cross your life."

"Yeah, son, I've been thinking about that, too. I thought about all of the guys we come in contact with every week at the golf club. On a busy Sunday afternoon, there's probably fifty we cross paths with, and we might see another fifty different ones the next Sunday."

"I stop just about every morning to get coffee. It's usually the same shop, but once a week or so, I may choose another one because of timing or another errand I am running. I see some of the same faces at each of those places. Most of them, I don't even know their names."

"I heard Detective Rivers tell you to begin making lists. Why don't you start with the casual places that you and Lana went together? As busy as the two of you have been in the last couple of years, there can't be too many of those. You go into the living room and start working on that list, and I will make us some meatloaf."

"Your meatloaf—I can't remember the last time I've eaten that. Maybe when I was still in college." Jared paused as he stood up from the kitchen chair he was seated in. The movement caused him to wince in pain. His father began to move toward him, but Jared held up his hand to stop him.

"I'm okay. This is nothing compared to how my heart feels. Your meatloaf will be just what the doctor ordered. I can't imagine more of a comfort food than that."

Jared tried to allow his mind to relax as he sat on his living room couch with a yellow legal pad in front of him. While he knew he should be focusing on coming up with a list of acquaintances, Jared's thoughts kept going back to Lana. All he could think about was where she was at that moment and what she may have to endure. He could not allow his thought process to think about the alternative. He was not ready to admit that his wife might already be deceased.

His eyes darted around the room. Only a few months earlier, they had bought the house. Lana had gone on a whirlwind spree of decorating. Previously, both their residences had been a mix-match of décor—hand-me-downs from family and friends or flea market finds. With their new home, their first home, Lana had wanted to buy all new furnishings. It did not surprise him that the living room in which he now sat looked like a page out of a furniture advertisement. Everything was carefully chosen and placed. It was so new that Jared wondered if all of the chairs had even been sat in yet. His broken heart wondered if they ever would be.

"THIS IS A LONG list, Jared. Perhaps, you could prioritize them in some way."

The following morning, Detective Rivers showed up at Jared's home to retrieve the list he had stayed up most of the night making.

"What? Would you like me to code it on a one-to-five scale of who is most likely to have wanted to take my wife? Should I grade on a curve as to who I thought had the most nerve?" Jared poured himself a cup of coffee after handing a cup to the detective. "I'm sorry. You don't deserve that. Making this list led me down some dark roads last night. I'm sick of dark roads. It's horrible to have to look at every person you have ever come in contact with as a potential threat."

"No apologies, Jared. It is an arduous and brutal task to put on someone. But you heard the profiler yesterday. This most likely is someone who has had at least casual contact with you or Lana. We can't question Lana's memory, so it is going to have to be yours. Can you remember her mentioning anyone or a situation that seemed out of the ordinary to her?"

"The last few months were a whirlwind. So much was changing in our lives."

"I understand. It is one of the reasons why this list is so crucial. I'm hoping that it will also trigger your memory regarding suspicious behavior." Detective Rivers stirred the cream into her coffee before taking a sip. "In her law practice, did she often deal with criminals?"

"Lana's primary focus was corporate law." Jared chuckled under his breath. "You might say that she dealt with a lot of criminals, but not the violent kind. Most of her cases involved business mergers or legal issues like that. Her firm doesn't deal much with the criminal side of law. At least, not that I am aware of." Jared paused to gulp down some of the steaming coffee. He had never been a huge drinker of the caffeinated elixir. He was more of a one cup in the morning kind of guy. Now, he imagined it might become a food group for him. "How do you even begin to look for a criminal like this?"

"Jared, it is a sea of details. The most difficult part could involve what you just said. Prior to abducting Lana, this person might not have been a criminal. He may have lived his entire life, which could be many decades, and never even had so much as a parking ticket. For Lana's potential for survival, that could be good. If he doesn't have a history of violence, it might make it more difficult for him to work up the nerve, so to speak, to hurt her. The physical harm that was inflicted on you is probably a part of the rage of envy that he feels. We must hope that her life is precious to him."

The detective stopped talking for a moment and looked at her phone. It gave Jared time to study her. Detective Rivers had what some might call the looks of an average attractive woman—pleasant features, pretty hair and a clear complexion. Mixed with the dark business suit, she looked like what he imagined was a textbook photo of a female detective in the police academy handbook. After multiple conversations, Jared had noticed something different about her though. Underneath the police exterior, Detective Rivers cared, and she was not afraid to allow a little emotion and a personal side to spill into her investigation. If she really cared about Lana, then perhaps she would not let the investigation flounder even if time became a factor.

"Please tell me more about the process. I want to understand what is happening. I want to help as much as I can."

"Our profiling began from the moment we were assigned. While I and Detective Oglesby are the lead investigators locally, you realize that this has become an FBI case. We are working together and under their supervision now. The scope of the investigation increases when a federal agency steps in. It has become a national search."

"Do kidnappers usually leave the area where the abduction took place?"

"With the abduction of children, that is often the case. In many of those cases, it involves a divorce situation and it may be the parent who does not have custody of the child who has taken the child. This parent goes 'on the run,' often travelling far away from the child's home. With adult situations, it is not as likely, but still possible. The FBI obviously thinks it is worth the effort, at least at this point, to advance a national search."

"What has been done on Lana's case thus far?"

"First, we begin with Lana. We look at the victim first. Who is she? Where does she work? Who does she associate with? We've had police officers interviewing everyone at Lana's firm as well as persons from offices adjacent to the firm. We also look at the person's actual profession. Some professions make people more vulnerable to abduction."

"What? What types of professions are more vulnerable?"

"Prostitution for one. Women who make their living selling themselves are the easiest victims as they put themselves into vulnerable positions every day. Their interaction with others is almost entirely made up of strangers. Many of them have little or no family, or are estranged from family members. They may not have close friendships or long-term ones, so it may take a while for anyone to miss them."

"That makes a lot of sense. Those women's lives are bad enough without having something like abduction hanging over them."

"It's true. Obviously though, Lana does not fall into that category. So we have to keep digging into deeper details of her life to try and find any clues as to how she might have interacted with her abductor. As soon as the investigation began, our agents confiscated her work computer and the computers here in your home."

"You're kidding me. I hadn't even noticed that our computers were gone." Jared hobbled toward the den that was off of the living room area. He returned to the room shaking his head. "It looks like we have been robbed."

"Your father was told. He let us into the house." The detective took a long drink of coffee before continuing. "Jared, your thought process has been consumed by shock and grief as well as the physical pain your body has endured. It will take you a while to begin functioning anywhere near normal again."

"I may never know what normal is again. It is an underappreciated state. The little things that make up each normal day are the best part of life." A heavy feeling came over him forcing Jared to sit back down on the stool at the nook. "I know that during those first few hours, at least, I was a suspect. I've seen enough movies over the years to understand that the husband is the first suspect. I've seen enough stories on television about murdered wives to understand why."

"All husbands are suspects when a violent crime is committed against their wives. Too often, husbands are the ones who commit the crimes. It became obvious fairly quickly as we were made aware of the extent of your injuries that it would have been hard for you to attack yourself in the manner that you were physically harmed. Only a serious psychopath would go to those lengths. You had nothing in your background that indicated a history of psychological problems. Everyone we interviewed who knew you both expressed sincere concern in how you would survive if the worst happens."

"The worst? Hasn't the worst already happened?" Jared poured the rest of his coffee down the drain. He opened the refrigerator and took out two bottles of water, handing the second one to the detective as she began to answer him.

"The worst meaning Lana being killed."

"I can't wrap my mind around that. I can't fathom a world without her. Yet, the worst to me would be that she would be held and tortured by some mad man for years. That's worse than her being dead. I'm not ready to accept either possibility. But, if I had to choose one, I would choose death for her. I cannot imagine any scenario of her being held for years, even if she was eventually released and produced a positive outcome. Continue with what you were telling me about how you try to develop a profile. I want to understand."

"As I was saying, we are reviewing Lana's emails, phone records, and other correspondence she received recently. Her law firm has been quite cooperative. I understand that even some of Lana's clients have offered to provide lists of employees who have recently interacted with her." Jared nodded as Detective Rivers continued. "There have been hundreds of tips from the public. We have interviewed many of your and Lana's friends; some have voluntarily come in to help with the investigation or the search. Jared, you may feel like you have been unable to do much while you were recovering. It's been amazing how many people have come forward desperate to do anything they can to help find her. Even your dry cleaner contacted the police."

"Mr. Chan." Jared smiled as he said the name. "He and his family are wonderful. Such a hardworking family."

"Mr. Chan is one smart and observant man. He went through his surveillance tapes and found segments that showed Lana coming in and out of the store over the last few weeks. He found two tapes that showed the same man standing behind Lana in line."

Jared felt an anxious feeling pass over him as he watched the detective's face. He wondered how many times he would have such a feeling before he would know where his Lana was.

"He told us who the man was, a regular customer of his. The man is a Marine who shipped out overseas a couple of days before Lana was taken." Detective Rivers' cell phone buzzed, causing her to look at it, push some buttons and return it to her pocket. "I am not telling you this to give you false hope. I am telling you to give an example of how important it can be for people to come forward. Someone knows something. The next tip could be the one that leads us to where Lana is. This is why we will work diligently with the news media to keep this story in the forefront. It doesn't have to be someone who knows Lana who can help us. It just has to be someone who recognizes her and feels like they have seen something, or someone who thinks they know the perpetrator."

"Is it more likely for a person to be abducted by someone they know?"

"Yes, it is rare for someone to be kidnapped by a stranger. Random killings are not rare, but taking someone and holding them hostage is usually a personal crime. As I mentioned before, in cases of child abduction, it is often an estranged parent. Many times when women are abducted, the perpetrator is an angry ex-boyfriend, spouse, or someone who the woman has turned advances from."

"My gut says that Lana would have told me about someone who might have been bothering her." Jared took in a deep breath as he rubbed his aching forehead. "But I also know that she would probably not want to worry me. She is an independent person. Lana would think that she could take care of the situation herself."

"Sadly, we independent women are like that. We forget that just because we have good men in our lives, it does not mean that all are that way. By nature, women are more trusting. It can be a dangerous flaw. What is even more likely is that the person may not have made their attentions or advances obvious. Lana might not have even realized at all, especially as busy as she has been in recent months. Unfortunately, that might have fueled the abductor's anger, as he may have felt ignored. Another factor to this is that abductors do not always look or act like criminals. As a general profile, most abductors of women are white males in their thirties or forties. Many do not have any previous criminal history. They often have had problems in relationships, in general, especially those with women. For many, abducting someone is their way of having power. It may be that they do not have much control over their own lives or much choice. They may be in jobs that do not offer opportunities for them to have authority, or they feel they have been held back in some way. Because of their lack of success in personal relationships, they may be socially isolated."

"Detective Rivers, I appreciate you being so frank with me. I need to understand this, even though every sentence that you utter makes me more afraid for Lana."

"We are going to be seeing a lot of each other. I hope that it is only for a short time, but it may be longer than any of us want to think about. Please feel free to call me Beth. We are going to be a team. There's no need for you to be formal with me." Beth smiled as she opened up the notebook Jared had noticed in front of her. After writing down a few words, she continued talking. "In this age of the internet, you can research all sorts of things online. You can find accurate and inaccurate information. You are a smart person. Once this really starts sinking in and your physical issues lessen, your mind is going to gain some clarity regarding what you are facing. Your love for your wife is going to make you want to do anything in your power to find her. I would rather that you have accurate answers to your questions. You need factual information from the perspective of this investigation, rather than half-truths or outright garbage that you can sometimes find online.

I don't want you acting hastily because of something that isn't true."

"How do you know me so well?" Jared gave her a half smile.

"You remind me of my own husband. From what I have initially gathered of your personality, you two could almost be brothers. Thomas rarely asks me about cases I am working on. He understands that I am dealing with confidential issues. He also values that our home is my safe place to get away from my day, so to speak."

"I've had a few friends who worked in public safety; somehow I imagine that you rarely completely get away from your day."

"That's true in many respects. It is what I signed on for. I always wanted to help people, to serve. I do try to 'turn off' as much as I can when I am home. It keeps me sane. Thomas helps me, most of the time. This is a very public case though, so the other night, he was asking me about it. He proceeded to tell me exactly what he would do if it was me who was taken. It was the most explicit conversation we have ever had. I knew then that you and I needed to have this chat. His approach was all wrong and was all about revenge. You've got to allow the investigation to proceed without your own perceived retaliation agenda. It will not help to get Lana back, and it could hurt the process. This is especially true when you are questioned by the media or making any public statements. If this abduction has its roots in coveting what you have, this guy will feed off your anger. It could make him hurt her. You being calm and controlled could have an effect of drawing him out. He may try to connect with you in person to see if it is all show."

"You mean that I could be bait."

"Yes. Does that concern you?"

"Not in the slightest. Bring it on."

Chapter Seven

"CHANNEL 10 EVENING NEWS, I'm Natalie Ryan. It's been one month since the frightening abduction of local attorney, Lana Kennedy, and the brutal beating of her husband, Jared, on Route 637. Investigators do not seem any closer to finding the perpetrator who committed this heinous act. It's as if Lana and her abductor disappeared into thin air. Let's go to Mattox Cleveland for the latest on the search for Lana."

Jared hit the off button on the remote before the young schoolboy face of the channel's newest reporter came on the screen. He knew what the reporter would say. He lived it twenty-four hours a day. Time dragged on like the grains of sand in an hourglass. Despite extensive investigations and interviews, as well as thousands of hours of searching by public safety and private citizens, they knew no more about where Lana might be than the night she was taken.

"I think it is time for you to go back to work, son." Jared's father was sitting on his own patio watching the snow softly fall from the November sky. "You need to get some structure to your life. You are not letting your body heal. You get up early in the morning and ride around searching past dark, even though there are hundreds of others doing the same. I'm worried about you."

"How is going back to work going to help me find Lana?"

"Well, for one thing, you will be able to pay your mortgage."

"I could care less about the house."

"But Lana did. She cared immensely. She searched for her dream home. She decorated it to look like a home out of *House & Garden*. Lana will be ticked at you when she returns and her beautiful house is gone."

"'When she returns.' I'm beginning to think that is an impossible dream."

"Did I ever tell you about how your mother and I got together?" Mr. Kennedy pointed to a chair opposite him on the patio. Jared sat down.

"You were on leave, I think, and you met her on a beach."

"That's how we met. That's not how we got together. I had a weekend pass and your mother was spending a few days at the same beach with her family. We played in the surf and took long walks under the stars. We had our first kiss on the very end of the fishing pier with the beam of the lighthouse shining down on us."

"Okay. Great story. It sounds like the beginning of an old movie. I'm ready to go to bed. I think I will bunk here." Jared stood up and began to walk toward the patio door.

"Sit back down, young man." With a deep sigh of tired, Jared returned to his seat. "I fell in love with your mother at first sight. It was like we connected in a way that, up until that point, I had only seen in the movies. Your parents were great romantics. I looked into your mother's eyes, and I saw the future. What I failed to think about was the present."

"What do you mean?"

"It was a different time. Men approached women. It wasn't considered polite for girls to give out too many details about themselves until they got to know a fellow better or he actually asked."

"So, what did you fail to ask Mom, her last name?" Jared chuckled under his breath. The silence that followed made him stop. "Oh, Dad, you didn't?"

"It wasn't quite that bad. It was mighty close. What was your mother's name before I married her?"

"Mary Smith." Jared stopped and considered what he had said. "That's a pretty common name. Never thought about that."

"Yes. There was nothing common about your mother

except her name. That really isn't the worst of it though. I didn't ask your mother where she lived. I meant to, but I didn't get to say goodbye on the Sunday morning that we were both leaving."

"Why didn't you get to say goodbye?"

"After we had gone out with the girls we had met, we decided to visit a bar on the boardwalk. We visited a little too long and overslept the next morning. By the time I reached the motel where your mother and her family were staying, they were gone."

"So, why didn't you just ask the motel for her address?"

"Jared, this didn't happen yesterday. This was forty years ago. People paid in cash and they didn't have to give their address. All I could find out was her father's first name."

"Grandpa John. Man, that's tough."

"Tough isn't the half of it. I knew that they were from some town about a hundred miles away, but I had no idea in which direction. I had the impossible task of finding the John Smith family from who-knows-where town."

"Wow. Since I know that you married Mom, I guess you made the impossible happen."

"It was a miracle. It was a simple, extraordinary miracle."

"Simple and extraordinary, isn't that a contradiction?"

"You won't be saying that when you hear how I found them. Go get your old man some hot chocolate with a nip of something in it for this cold snowy night. I will tell you my story."

Jared returned to the patio a few minutes later with two steaming mugs of cocoa and a blanket for his father's legs.

"I don't want your knees to lock up because Mr. Arthur got cold."

"Thank you, son. With that beating you took, you are going to know Mr. Arthur yourself one day. He will find those places to reside when you cross into the second half of your life."

"Finish your story, Dad."

"As I said, I had no idea where your mother lived and a name like Smith didn't help much. Your grandparents vacationed at that beach every summer. Sometimes they would stay a couple of weeks I was told. Your mom had made friends with one of the local girls; her name was Jilly, and she had been dating my buddy, Hank. Jilly wasn't much help at first. She said that she and your mother never corresponded through the year; they were just summer friends. We had to ship back out that evening. I thought I would never see your mother again. It was one of the saddest days of my life."

Jared took a big drink of the cocoa. He wished he had put more scotch in his mug. He wished he had spent more time sleeping the night before.

"We shipped out and a couple of weeks passed. I thought a lot about that pretty girl with the cute giggle. I committed her face to memory. Realistically, I resigned myself to the fact that I would probably never see her again. Until one day about three weeks later, Hank got a letter from Jilly."

"Wait a minute. Hank and Jillian, my godparents—is that who you are talking about?"

"Those are the ones. They had to be your godparents. You wouldn't have existed if it hadn't been for them."

"How come I have never heard this story before?"

"Oh, son, there are tons of stories you have never heard. A child is rarely interested in their parents' lives before they existed. I'm sure that the four of us talked about this in your presence when you and their kids were young. You all tuned us out."

"I suppose that is true. Keep talking, old man, you've peeked my interest."

"The letter to Hank included a picture, but it wasn't just of Jilly. It was one of her and your mother, and they were sitting on the hood of your grandfather's car. The photo showed the license plate."

"Oh, my goodness! That is a stroke of luck. Please tell me that there was a DMV back then." Jared gave his father a smirk, and Mr. Kennedy shook his head and rolled his eyes.

"Yes, smarty, there was. We found someone who was willing to help us. Agencies were far freer with giving out personal information then, thank heavens. As soon as I got the address, I wrote the longest, sappiest letter you would ever want to read. Mary wrote me back, and, as they say, the rest is history."

"That's a great story, Dad. But I don't see the parallel to my situation with Lana."

"Son, there was really no reason that I should have ever seen Mary Smith again. All of the signs were against it. It was a hopeless situation. All it took to change that was one person going out of their way with a tiny piece of information. It made all the difference in the world."

"ARE YOU THE man who lost his wife?"

Jared swallowed the bite of sandwich he was eating in the deli down the street from his office. It went down the wrong way, and Jared began coughing and drinking water to dislodge it as the person who had asked the question watched him.

"I have a neighbor who has acted very strangely ever since this woman went missing." The elderly woman standing in front of him unfolded a flyer with Lana's photo. Thousands of the flyers were posted everywhere within a two-hour radius of the abduction site. "I have carried this flyer with me everywhere since it happened. I think you are the man I've seen on the news talking about her. The other day it occurred to me that it could be my strange neighbor who took her. I've seen a woman standing at the window on the very top floor, and she has motioned to me. From a distance, she looks like the woman in the flyer."

Three months had passed without any substantial leads on the whereabouts of Lana. Physical searches of the area had ceased six weeks earlier as volunteers began to dwindle. While there had been hundreds of tips reported, none of them were even remotely promising. Jared could not help but wonder, as he tried to clear his throat, if this was just another dead end.

"Can you tell me where you live, ma'am?"

"No, I can't do that. You are a stranger. For all I know, you could be a kidnapper." The woman scowled and shook her finger. "Don't you follow me."

"But, ma'am, you approached me and said your neighbor might have my wife. What do you expect me to do?"

"Well, I just don't know. I didn't plan to see you here. I looked over from where I was sitting, and I saw you and before I knew what I was doing, I was talking to you. I guess I didn't think this through. I don't know what to do."

"Why don't you sit down, and I will call one of the police officers who is working on the case. Would that be okay?"

"Yes, I guess so." The woman looked around before sitting down in the chair across from Jared. "I will need to see that it is a real officer before I will talk to him."

Jared took in a deep breath and resisted the urge to roll his eyes. He had to have patience. Beth had told him over and over again. People did not always make sense when they thought they had a lead. Their logic regarding the situation might not match his. In this case, this woman's logic was not even in the same room as his. He had to be patient.

"Hello, Beth. This is Jared." The woman kept a close watch on Jared as he made the call. "I'm here at the corner deli near my office with a lady who says that she thinks her neighbor might have Lana. Would you like to talk to her?"

Jared handed the woman his phone. At first, she shooed it away, but he kept holding it out to her.

"Hello." The woman began talking. "Are you sure you are a real police officer? I don't know many women cops around here." The woman listened to Beth. Whatever was being said, must have been convincing because the woman nodded her head several times, and then said yes before handing the phone back to Jared. "She wants to talk to you."

"Beth?"

"I've convinced this woman that I will come down there in a squad car with a male uniformed officer and talk to her. Call your office and tell them you need to take a long lunch. Don't leave her alone. I know she sounds a little crazy to you. Put it out of your mind. Sometimes it is people like her who have the most credible information. Sit tight."

"Thanks for agreeing to stay." The woman still looked a little leery of Jared. "Where are my manners? My name is Jared Kennedy." Jared held out his hand. She looked from his face to his hand and then back to his face before shaking it.

"I'm Dixie Land."

Jared's eyes grew big as he stifled a laugh. Quickly covering his mouth and faking a cough.

"Go ahead and laugh, I've heard it all before. I should have known better than to ever go on a date with a man named Land."

For the first time since she had first spoken to him, the woman smiled. In that moment, Jared realized that perhaps she was not as strange as he thought. Perhaps, it was just a strange thing for anyone to approach someone with information as horrible as what had happened to Lana and him. Beth was right; he needed to be more patient and understanding.

"Dixie, may I call you Dixie?" The woman nodded. "May I buy you a cup of coffee?"

Thirty minutes later, Beth arrived with another officer in an unmarked car. After introductions, Beth sent Jared back to his office. He impatiently waited for almost three hours before he heard from her.

"We've gathered as much preliminary information as we could. We will keep the house under surveillance until we can obtain a warrant."

"Beth, am I hearing you correctly? You think there is a possibility that this is a real lead?"

"Jared, it is hard to tell. But Mrs. Land had some serious examples of her neighbor's behavior that should give us enough reason for a judge to issue a search warrant. Don't read too much into what I am about to say, but it is one of the best leads we have had thus far. I will be in touch."

After working late, Jared stopped to get some takeout before going home. While it had been a mild winter, the days had still become short. The darkness had curtailed Jared's late night searches. Tonight was different though; he could not go home and face that empty house without wandering up and down some streets. Despite her warning, Beth's words had given him a little hope. It was a precious commodity that he wanted to keep growing, nurturing, on the chance it might turn into something real.

He found himself driving up and down the streets within blocks of their home. Why he was looking in this neighborhood was beyond his own comprehension. He let his mind take him on autopilot most days; it was the numbness that had become his new normal. While sitting at a stop sign, Jared looked around to the houses on each side of the street. He realized he had stopped in front of the home of Morris Dillion, the co-worker from another department who he had taken home one day. The golden glow of lamplight filtered out from the front windows. Jared wondered about Morris. He knew little of the man and did not know whether or not he was married or had a family. He imagined that the man was having a normal evening in his home. Jared felt a surge of envy. He realized that he had started to covet the life of another person and for a split second, Jared wondered if he had begun to understand the criminal before he understood the crime.

"JARED, YOU HAVE to focus on that this was a positive outcome for another family." Beth Rivers sat across from him in the same café where Mrs. Land had approached him a week earlier. "The young woman was a runaway when she became missing several years ago. Now she has been safely returned to her family."

Mrs. Land's instincts were correct regarding the strange behavior of her neighbor. He was indeed holding someone hostage, in a sense, in his home. The man had picked up a young girl in her mid-teens a couple of years earlier. While not exactly imprisoned physically, the now-young woman was afraid to leave for fear that he would come after her, or she would encounter someone worse when she was on the streets again. The woman was returned to her family, and the man was arrested.

"I'm happy for the woman's family." Jared's stoic reply showed little emotion. "I'm sure that they had given up hope of finding her alive by now. I'm beginning to understand that feeling."

"Jared, you can't give up."

"Beth, I will never give up. I promised Lana infinity and that's exactly what she will get. But reality is a cruel friend. It forces you to face what you don't want to think about. We are closing in on six months. I've read the statistics.

Lana's disappearance isn't news anymore. Finding this young woman is the new news. I'm not sure that people are still looking for my wife."

"I am. We are."

"I know that." Jared shook his head up and down in a repetitive manner. "I appreciate it. Lana always excelled at everything. It's no wonder that the person who chose to take her needed to excel at hiding."

"Jared, your keen thoughts are getting stranger." Beth nodded as the server refreshed her iced tea. "Try to keep positive as much as you can. There will be more leads that will be followed up on. Not all of them will turn into as positive outcomes as this one."

"Positive for someone." Jared drank the last of his coffee and picked up the bill.

"The next positive could be for you."

"I want a positive for Lana." Jared rose. He closed his eyes and took a deep breath. "I want whatever is positive for her. I don't matter. I want her to be safe."

DAYS TURNED INTO weeks, then weeks became months. Despite the slow pace at which Jared thought the time went by, months turned into years. Leads that had come in daily in the beginning, now barely trickled in monthly.

It became harder to even get the local media to give Lana's story anniversary coverage. Years were quickly a decade. Jared began to accept that it might be infinity before he knew what had happened to his love.

after

Chapter Eight

"Jared, come on in, son, I want you to meet my new neighbor."

It was the second Sunday of the month which meant that Jared would be playing golf with his father. Instead of meeting at the course, as they normally did, his father had suggested that Jared stop by and pick him up. He thought that was strange. As Jared got the first glimpse of his father's new young female neighbor, Jared had a sinking feeling he now knew why.

"I let Jared drive me around the golf course once a month. Sometimes, he plays a little, it rarely amounts to much." Mr. Kennedy winked at the young woman before giving his son a raised eyebrows look.

The woman gave Jared a knowing smile. She seemed

to understand why she was there as well. She began to rise from the chair she was sitting in at the breakfast nook.

"I better get out of your way then."

"No, just a minute. Karin, this is my son, Jared Kennedy. Jared, this is my new neighbor, Karin Tyler."

Jared extended his hand to the woman. She was average height with dark brown hair that fell just past her shoulders. Dressed in shorts and a polo shirt, Jared noticed that she had splotches of white paint on her outfit.

"It's nice to meet you, Jared. In case you are wondering, I'm becoming one with my new home by painting myself as well as the banisters of my front porch."

"That's what I call getting acclimated to your new surroundings." Jared smiled as he shook Karin's hand. "I'm sure you will enjoy being the youngest person in the neighborhood. Probably the youngest by several decades."

"Yes. I believe I will be. I inherited the house behind your father's. It was my grandparents' home."

"Oh, yes. The Sinclairs. Dad told me that Mrs. Sinclair passed away a few months ago. I was sorry to hear that."

"Thank you. She was ninety-three and still lived alone. Grammie lived an amazing life."

"Dorothy was a WASP in World War II, Jared." Mr. Kennedy handed Jared and Karin bottles of water from the refrigerator. "She had some amazing stories. That's how she met your grandfather, isn't it, Karin?"

"Yes."

"I'm sorry. I guess I should know my history better. What did you say she was?" A confused look crossed Jared's face as he unscrewed the cap of the bottle.

"No worries, Jared. It's not featured in too many history books. I probably wouldn't know if it wasn't for all of my grandmother's stories. My grandmother was a WASP. That stands for Women Airforce Service Pilots. She was one of over a thousand women who were trained to fly aircraft in the early 1940s during World War II. After the attack on Pearl Harbor, male pilots were in short supply. There was a need for more pilots who could deliver the trainer aircraft to flight schools in the South." Karin paused and took a drink of water.

"That is quite impressive."

"Having a grandmother who served made it an interesting topic to me."

"You speak quite eloquently. You should be a teacher. You could inspire future generations." Jared watched as smiles were exchanged between Karin and his father.

"Karin is a teacher, Jared. She teaches elementary school. Fifth grade, if I remember correctly."

"Guilty as charged." Karin grabbed her bottle of water and stood up. "But that is not my job today. I need to get back to painting. Jared, it was nice to meet you. Your father has spoken of you several times. Mr. Kennedy, I will be seeing you through the backyard later." Karin walked toward the door.

"Great to meet you too, Karin. I really enjoyed hearing about the WASP program."

"Karin, I will come over later this evening and inspect your painting work after I let this tall guy drive me around the golf course a few times."

Karin smiled and waved before the door closed behind her.

"You mentioned your new neighbor a few days ago. I never imagined that she wouldn't be on Medicare." Jared picked up his father's golf bag as they began to walk out to the garage. "Now, I know why you wanted me to pick you up."

"You know that I wouldn't meddle in your life. It's just that—"

"No, it's okay. For once, I don't think I mind the introduction. Karin seems very nice—intelligent, funny. You know, it's been so hard to imagine myself with anyone else. I really was planning to be one of those 'till death do you part' guys. There was no death, at least that I know about." Jared paused and felt the familiar tightness in his chest that occurred when he allowed himself to think about it. "Lana is gone. I know that one day I need to accept that."

"Jared, when Lana was first taken, I never imagined that ten years would pass without some resolution. I really thought that one day she would either be found alive or there would be evidence to the contrary." Mr. Kennedy got into the driver's seat of Jared's vehicle. "I hate seeing you so lonely. I wouldn't dream of interfering in your life. You're a grown man; you can find your own dates. I met Karin several times while her grandmother was still living. Always thought she was a lovely person and was pleased to learn that she was single. But Karin was living about an hour away then. When she decided to get a job here and move into her grandmother's home, I decided it was a sign this dynamic young woman should meet you. If nothing else, I could see you two becoming friends."

"I believe we could, Dad. Perhaps I need to stop by for one of your backyard dinners with Karin sometime."

"I WAS HAPPY TO hear from you, Jared."

"I thought we've had enough chaperoned dates in Dad's backyard."

Jared nodded to the server who brought their beverages. A month had passed since he first met Karin. Since then, he would stop by once a week and have impromptu dinners with her and his father on the patio that stood between the two properties.

"Like I've said before, I didn't know your father planned to introduce us."

"Dad's a sly one. He's bad at taking his own advice though. My mother passed away while I was still in high school. He's been a widower for twenty years. He's barely dated any ladies past a third or fourth date." Jared watched as a puzzled look crossed Karin's face. She quickly looked down at her menu. "What? You look like you know something that might contradict that statement."

"Oh, no. I'm sure I don't." Karin gave Jared what he perceived to be a nervous smile. "Do you eat here often? I just love Thai food, but I always order the same thing."

"Stop avoiding my question. You suggested this place. What do you know about my father's dating habits that I do not?"

"I'm really not at liberty to say."

"Okay, if you don't tell me, I will just make something up. I'll tell Dad that you told me he was dating Mrs. Salecki across the street." Karin's eyes bugged out. "No way. You're not telling me that my father is dating Mrs. Salecki?"

"No, I am not telling you that." Karin raised her eyebrows and tilted her head. "I never said that."

"How long has this been going on?" Karin held up two fingers. "Two weeks?"

"Two weeks? Really, Jared? I probably wouldn't know about it, if it had just been two weeks."

"Two months is quite a long time to hide it from your son."

"Oh, and you have never in your life hid anything from your father." Karin shook her head as the server returned. After giving their orders, she resumed talking to Jared. "Two months is a short time in this situation as well."

"No. This can't be right. My father has been dating Margaret Salecki for two years? Why wouldn't he tell me that?"

"Because he has been concerned about you. My grandmother told me about what happened to your wife. Your father feels guilty that he has someone and you don't."

"I never dreamed Dad would feel that way. I honestly just thought that all of these years without my Mom, he just got used to being a bachelor." Jared paused and looked at the tables around them. "Mrs. Salecki seems like a nice lady. I hope he is happy."

"I think he is. I barged in on one of their evenings together when I locked myself out of my house a couple of weeks ago. I remembered that my grandmother had given him a spare key and hoped he still had it. They were eating pizza and watching a movie. They looked really cute together."

"That makes me happier than you can realize. I may still have to give him a hard time though. Maybe we can go on a double date with them sometime."

Jared looked into Karin's eyes. The words had come out before he thought about what he was saying. In that moment, he realized that, perhaps, he was ready to move on as well.

"I would like that."

"It's been a while since I've heard from you. How have you been doing?"

Jared waited for almost an hour in a hard chair in the foyer of the police headquarters to see Beth Rivers. Many people had passed by him during that time. He wondered about the circumstances that brought them there. Did any of them have a story like his?

During the weeks and months after Lana's abduction, he had known Detective Rivers as the lead officer on the case. In the years since, she had moved up in rank, but she made sure to keep up with any new leads or information. Jared had gotten to know her as Beth, the person. He became acquainted with her husband, Thomas, and would attend little league games where their young son, Parker, was a star player. He sat in the stands and cheered on Parker's team. Few sitting around them would dream how they became friends—for better and worse, they had become a part of each other's lives.

"I've been good, Beth. How are Thomas and Parker?"

"Parker broke his arm right before the season started. That's why I haven't harassed you with his game schedule. Thomas is hoping that the cast will be off before soccer starts. What have you been up to?"

"Well, believe it or not, I've actually begun seeing someone."

"Oh, Jared, I'm so happy to hear that. I worry about you being alone."

"Well, so did my Dad. He hooked me up with his new neighbor. He did a good job. Karin is a fabulous person. She's a fifth grade teacher. We like a lot of the same things. We ride bikes together in the evenings and cook strange recipes on the weekends. I feel comfortable with her. I think this might work out. I would like for you and Thomas to meet her."

"It's healthy. It's time."

"Doesn't mean that I've given up though. Any new tips come in after the TV station did that anniversary segment?"

"A few. One of Mr. Luigi's nieces came in for his funeral."

"I heard that he had passed. He was way up in his nineties."

"Yes. The niece, actually I believe she is a great-niece, worked there for a few months and left the area. Her last week was just a few days after Lana was abducted. She saw the segment while she was here for the funeral. Something clicked in her memory."

"Forgive me. It seems rather strange that she would remember something after all of these years."

"I understand your doubt, especially after all the time that has passed. But it was what she remembered that seemed important."

Jared watched closely as Beth pulled out a file from the stack on her desk.

"On the day she came in, Parker was sick and I was at home with him. One of the newer detectives called me after she left. He said that she remembered something he thought I would want to look at."

"Look at? I don't understand."

"The woman told him that on the evening that Lana was abducted she waited on a man who sat at a table within view of where you and Lana sat. She remembered you two from when you used to eat there while you were students."

"She remembered us? That doesn't make sense. That was so many years previous."

"She was a child then. Her mother worked at the restaurant. As a little girl, she had a crush on you." Beth paused and smiled. "You used to joke with her and pull her pigtails."

"Sofia." A rush of memories hit Jared. "Sometimes she sat with us and did her homework. Sofia was waiting tables the night Lana and I were there?"

"Yes. Apparently, she had been working at Luigi's for a few months and was getting ready to move to go to college. He said she needed to earn more money before she could go."

"I remember Sofia's mother worked long hours at the restaurant. I think she was a single parent."

"Sofia mentioned that her mother became ill, and she postponed going to college until she was better. Her uncle gave her a job to help her get on her feet and even gave her some money for college when she left."

"So, of course, she came back for his funeral." Jared paused as his mind thought back to the little girl. "What did she remember?"

"She remembered seeing the two of you that night and how happy you were. Sofia said that she wanted to stop and talk to you both that evening, but they were shorthanded and very busy. The time flew by and you were gone." Beth looked down at the file of papers. "When she saw the TV segment, there was a clip with you speaking and saying that you would love Lana until infinity. It made Sofia remember something about that night. It was this."

Beth handed Jared a sheet of paper. There were several infinity symbols drawn on it.

"I don't understand."

"Sofia said that she waited on a man that night that drew infinity symbols all over the paper placemat."

Jared swallowed and took a deep breath. A feeling of anger that had taken years for him to learn to control began to rise like a flame within him. His mind flashed back to the moment when he saw Lana's hand pressed against the glass as the abductor drove the Jeep away. It was an image that had awakened him more nights than he could count.

"You mean to tell me that he sat there a few feet away from us and drew the symbol that represented our relationship?" Jared stood up and slammed his fist into the filing cabinet. The impact was so hard that two officers burst through the door to see what was wrong.

"It's okay, guys. Jared just needed to let out a little aggression. He's going to sit down now." Beth gave Jared a stern look. He shook out his hand as he went back to his seat. The officers kept their eyes on him until he was seated. "Everything is fine. You can go." The officers backed out of the doorway.

"I'm sorry."

"You've worked so hard to deal with your emotions. It's natural to be angry. We've got to use that energy for something productive." Jared nodded as Beth continued. "What this new information tells me is that this guy really knew a lot about your relationship. Back when we were first investigating, we focused on it being someone who coveted the relationship you had. We theorized that it was probably a man who was more likely to have known you or the two of you together. This bit of information tells us that this guy knew about the significance of infinity symbols. That could mean that it was really someone you or Lana knew. Someone who had interacted with one or both of you enough to know things that were personal and unique. This man didn't draw hearts, he drew infinity symbols. He knew the intimacy of that symbol."

"Were you able to get a description from Sofia? Was there enough for a sketch artist to work with her?"

"It was about as much as we had from the surveillance video. He had on a hat and did not look up at her much. It was dark in the corner where he was sitting."

"So, basically nothing more than the guy knew about the infinity symbol. That doesn't narrow it down much. I mean that could really be either of us. When we were in college, Lana would unconsciously draw the symbol on all of her papers. I occasionally noticed while she was working on cases that she would draw them on other pieces of paper, not her work. Sometimes she might be reading briefs in the evening and making out a grocery list, I would see her doodling on the list." Jared rubbed his sore hand and cleared his throat.

"What about you? Did you ever draw the symbol on things?"

"No, I'm not a doodler by nature. I do have a wooden infinity symbol paperweight on my desk at work. It was a gift from Lana when I got my first job after college. You've seen the one on a chain that hangs in my car from the rearview mirror."

"I can't remember. Was the Jeep the vehicle that you drove or Lana's?"

"It was Lana's. I've always driven a Honda. Cary Kennedy is a Honda man." Jared paused as he watched Beth. She was making notes and seemed lost in her own thoughts. "After all these years, Beth, do you think there is any possibility that Lana is still alive?" Jared had asked Beth the question many times over the years and always got the same answer.

"Jared, I'm not going to sugarcoat it. If she is still alive, you might wish that she wasn't."

"Finally. You've given me a straight answer." Jared stood up and walked toward the door. "Since you have surprised me, I will do the same. I hope she is gone. I hope it was swift and painless, and she did not have to spend even one day with that psychopathic piece of—" Jared stopped himself. "Thank you for never giving up, Beth. I appreciate your understanding more than you will ever know. But we've got to find him. We've got to get justice for Lana. Infinity isn't up yet."

"You and Karin have been dating how long?" Jared's co-worker Vince stopped by his office on a Friday afternoon.

"About a year. Remember, I brought Karin with me to Isaiah's retirement party a few months after we started dating."

"It doesn't seem like that long. Yet, in some ways, it seems like she has always been a part of your life."

"We certainly have developed a strong relationship. I don't know if I would say that it seems like always though."

"Man, I'm sorry. I shouldn't have said that. I am incredibly glad though to see my best friend beginning to enjoy life again and allowing himself to think about opening his heart."

"Karin has made that part easy. She even encourages

me to talk about Lana. This will probably sound ludicrous, but it's almost like Lana sent her to me." Jared shook his head as he listened to his own words, realizing what they meant.

"It's not a bit crazy. With the connection you two had, I would not be surprised if Lana reached out to you from another realm and guided your life." Vince paused and put his hand on Jared's shoulder. "It was obvious to everyone that her love was that strong. She would find a way to keep reaching you. Maybe Karin is a sign from her that it's time for you to move on. Lana may be telling you something that a police investigation never will."

"That's a profound statement coming from you. I've got to admit that I've thought about that. I really have. You know, there have been a few other women who have entered my life. Some of them because of lame matchmaking skills." Jared smiled at Vince and shook his head. "Nothing ever even remotely clicked with any of them."

"It was sad, bro. A couple of them were beauty pageant friends of my sister."

"The girls were attractive, but their souls weren't nearly as beautiful as my Lana's."

"So Karin has a beautiful soul."

"She does, man. I think there's a reason she's found mine. When you think about the chances of us meeting, it's kind of crazy. I can't imagine that our paths would have ever crossed were it not for the fact that her grandparents were my father's neighbors for so many years. Even at that, I never once met her while they were alive. And what thirtysomething young woman moves into a retirement neighborhood?"

"The one who was destined to revive Jared Kennedy's heart."

"Yeah, maybe so. But, since the first day I met her, I have had this feeling that there is something bigger to this than it seems."

"Well, I guess you are going to have to keep moving forward with it and find out what that something is."

"The only problem is that to really move forward, I have to end something."

"Didn't you tell me that Detective Rivers said enough time has passed for Lana to be declared dead?"

"Yes, I think in most cases the minimum time is seven years. She told me that before then, she was sure that a judge would declare us divorced if I wanted to remarry."

"But you don't want to do that."

"The whole concept is just so foreign to me." Jared took in a deep breath. "I never expected to be here. Even after a decade has passed, sometimes it still doesn't seem real."

"I noticed a while ago that you stopped wearing your wedding band."

"I didn't think it was fair to Karin for her to be dating a man who wore one. I guess that was my first step in trying to think of a life with her. It was a hard step." Jared felt his finger where the band had been. "It's funny though. After I took it off, there was something peaceful about the feeling that came over me."

"You know me, I'm not one to talk about feelings and stuff very much. I spent most of my life not thinking, much less believing, in love or connections between people, or anything really past what I could see and hear in front of my own face." Vince shook his head and frowned. "I lost a lot of good years and probably special people just living in the moment and not thinking about anything deeper than the next girl I was going to meet or the next fun weekend I was going to have. Then, I met this guy named Jared who had his whole life together. I sat on the other side of this cubicle and eavesdropped on his conversations with the most wonderful girl in the world. I realized that there was something bigger than me."

"I remember that guy. He got on my nerves." Jared smiled at his friend. "I've seen him change a lot though."

"Yeah, he's changed. Hopefully for the better. He watched you seal the deal on this incredible relationship, and then his heart broke with you as it was taken away. I kept thinking that it was going to break you. That you would turn into some cynical bitter person who turned his back on life. But that never happened. You were angry, darkly angry. You were hurt, on levels that I doubt most people ever feel. Through it all, I've always seen hope in you. There's been a sliver of light carrying you forward. I think that light was Lana when she was physically a part of your life. I think that light is still her, in some other form. You are as bound to her now as you were on your wedding day. Falling in love with Karin isn't going to change that. I think it just might make your relationship with her even more special. Lana taught you how to love unconditionally, even if one of those conditions is the ultimate separation."

"Vince, I think those may be the wisest words I have heard. I never thought about it quite that way. There were times that I wanted so bad to settle into that depressed rage that hits me sometimes. I literally felt something tugging at me to get me out of it. You may have just explained it. When you have the brilliance of infinity on your side, how can you stay in the dark?"

Chapter Nine

"YOU CAN DRIVE A BUS?"

"I had a lot of time to fill after Lana was taken. So, I took up a hobby, a side job to fill the time." A darkness fell over Jared's face as if a curtain had been drawn. "I could pour myself into work at the firm during the week. Long days of intricate details regarding clients' accounts, working after hours studying trends, then I would go home tired. Quick meals in front of late night television, or the occasional visit over to Dad's, or with friends. The weekends were another story. Most of my friends were paired off in couples or starting families. I was happy for them. I was unhappy for me. I couldn't hang around with them for any length of time. It was too hard watching them create the life that I knew I was supposed to have." Jared paused and looked out of the window.

"Indescribably difficult at any point in your life." Karin filled the silence of his pause. "You don't seem to be the kind of person who wallows in their grief though. Jared Kennedy is a doer, someone who will find something to fill the time."

"You've gotten to know me quite well. That is exactly what I did. I'd always been a good driver. It was a skill that came naturally to me. A co-worker told me about her family's business. They organized trips for senior citizens and transported them on big buses—motor coaches is the industry term. They never had enough drivers for the weekend trips. I got my CDL license and applied. I spent several years driving almost every weekend. In the beginning, every Saturday morning was a new adventure. There were so many different trips that for the first couple of months, there was no duplication. I was always driving the one-day or two-day excursions, so it didn't interfere with my job. As the years passed, I began driving the routes that I enjoyed best, often with groups of people I had driven before. I could be on the open road and away from the reality of my life. It was an escape."

"Why did you stop?"

"I met you. I started not wanting to escape anymore."

Karin reached over and took Jared's hand. They were sitting at a picnic table in a park near Karin's apartment. Afternoon picnics were now a regular Sunday ritual.

"I'm glad you don't want to escape anymore."

"I hope it doesn't bother you for me to talk about Lana. I don't want you to feel uncomfortable."

"Absolutely not." Karin squeezed his hand. "I remember when it happened. My grandmother told me about it. I was living close enough to follow the story initially. Then, as time passed, the whole country was following the story. There were thousands of people looking for Lana and hoping for a happy outcome. I remember consciously thinking about her each time I saw someone who remotely matched her description." Karin paused and Jared looked into her eyes. He saw compassion radiating from them. "As much as I love having you as a part of my life, I wish you would have found her. I wish this was not how you came to me. You talk about her every day. Every single day. Keep her alive. Never stop looking. Never stop hoping."

"She may still be alive. It is what torments me the most. If I knew that she was dead, I could accept it. I could grieve. I'm afraid I will never stop looking for her. I've just stopped expecting to find her." Jared's mind raced with tortured memories. "I've laid awake more nights than I care to remember imagining what happened to her. People say that death is the worst thing to go through, the worst loss. I disagree. There are things worse than death. I believe this was worse for her. I know it was worse for me."

Jared looked across the park and saw a couple playing with their children. Screams of delight could be heard as the father swung his young son in the air. Jared's heart filled with longing, followed by anger.

"You are grinding your teeth again." Karin's comment brought him back to their conversation. "Dr. Sanchez is going to start making you wear your mouth guard during the day."

"It's a wonder I have any teeth left. I'm just not conscious that I am doing it anymore. It does beat the punching the wall therapy I used to do." Jared shook his hand out as if he had just hit something. "Don't look so shocked, I'd like to tell you that I am joking. I'm not. I did start punching something a little less hard. I took up kickboxing."

"You can change the tone of the conversation on a dime." Karin shook her head and smiled. "Back to the bus driving. So, you could drive the bus for our field trip to the aquarium?"

"Absolutely. I have kept my CDL current. I can probably even get you a good deal on the cost with the company I used to work for. They have begged me to start driving again. I could donate my driving fee."

"That would be wonderful." Jared watched as Karin's face lit up. It was like an elixir to the darkness in his heart. "The kids have done so much fundraising, but a few of them don't have the resources to contribute to the costs. Some of the teachers were going to make up the difference."

"I would love to help you and the children. It would not be a problem at all. Besides, it would get me some brownie points with one special teacher I've been trying to impress." Jared winked and squeezed her hand as he rose from the table and took their lunch trash to the garbage can.

"I know. I've been worried about losing you to Mrs. Dimarrio. I just cannot compete with her." Karin scowled as she gathered their cups and plates and put them back into the picnic basket.

"Don't beat yourself up about it, babe. You really can't compete with her. A thirtysomething woman like you just doesn't stand a chance with my first grade teacher. She was my first love. I can't help it. I can write my name because of Mrs. Dimarrio. You can't top that, babe."

"I know. Young teachers have it rough. She's been teaching for over forty years. You can't compete with that."

Jared and Karin walked hand in hand back to the parking lot. In front of them on the path, were two teenage girls. One of them had short hair. There was an infinity symbol tattooed to the nape of her neck. A feeling of sadness quickly returned to Jared. He let go of Karin's hand as he left the pathway and briskly walked toward his vehicle.

"What's wrong?" Karin caught up with him as he placed the basket in the trunk. "What happened to you just now? I could feel your mood change."

"It's not you, Karin." Jared closed the hatch and stared at the glass in front of him. A flash of memory streaked in front of his eyes as he saw Lana's hand on the glass. "Some memories are hard to shake. They visit me at the strangest moments."

"Tell me." Karin encircled him from behind, resting her head on the middle of his back. "I want to understand."

"Sometimes, I think you would be better off without me. I have too much baggage." Jared let out a big sigh and shook his head. He turned around and kissed Karin on the forehead as he embraced her.

"I'll help you carry it. I'm strong. I work out three times a week." A brief smile crossed her face before her expression returned to a serious one. "You don't have to keep it inside. I want to help you."

"The young girl in front of us on the path, the one with the short hair, she had an infinity symbol tattoo on her neck."

"I saw that. I've also seen you draw the symbol several times and it's also hanging from a chain inside your vehicle."

"Really? You've seen me draw it?"

Jared tried to think of when it might have occurred. He knew that he had a habit of absentmindedly doodling the shape. His grief counselor had told him years ago that it might be a tool to help his mind relax and get some of the emotion out. He did not think he ever did it when others were watching.

"Enough times that I have remembered it. I haven't figured out if it means something to you or you just like the swirly lines. It's the only thing I've seen you draw."

"Well, I will settle that debate you are having in your head."

Jared opened the door and Karin got into the vehicle. As he walked around the back to get into the driver side, he allowed his hand to touch the glass. He had started doing that a few weeks after Lana was taken. In a small way, it made him feel connected to her. He wondered why no one had asked him about that habit.

"The infinity symbol had an important meaning to me and Lana." Jared turned the ignition on and rolled down the front windows to let the interior heat escape from the sun's baking. "It all started because Lana doodled that symbol. It's ironic to know that I now do the same."

"I DON'T THINK I studied enough." The girl behind him leaned over his shoulder from her desk. She was so close that he could feel her breath on his neck. It gave him chills on the warm day all the way down to his toes. He thought he caught a whiff of baby shampoo. "My roommate says that over half of Mr. Bovender's class fails each semester. The administration is supposedly investigating it. That doesn't do us much good right now though."

"Maybe it won't be so bad. It's the first test of the semester. He probably won't start off with a hard one."

Jared's first class on Tuesdays and Thursdays was Economics. The professor had a notorious reputation for being tough. Even though it was the beginning of his freshman year at the university, Jared had already heard the horror stories. Several older guys in his dorm had cringed when he told them who he had for the class.

"Maybe this will be our lucky day." He smiled at the pretty girl as she leaned back into her seat. Jared could not remember her name.

"Hey, Lana, are we still meeting at the library this afternoon to work on the history assignment?" A tall boy who lived down the hall from Jared turned around from the row next to them. He gave Jared a piercing look. The look reminded him of Lurch from *The Addams Family*.

"Yes, I guess we can still do that. Thanks for reminding me."

The guy smiled and raised his eyebrows to Jared as he turned around. Jared decided that he did not like that guy. Now, he knew her name was Lana. Maybe he could get a study date with her himself, and maybe it could lead to a real one.

"You have thirty minutes to complete the test. It is open book." The professor laughed. It was a snorting sound. "Not that it will help most of you. You may now begin."

Time inched by. Jared did not think that the test was too hard. That was a sure sign he was failing it. Every few minutes, he would hear Lana tapping a pencil on her desk. As one by one, those around them finished, they took their papers to the front and left the room, but Jared could feel the tension growing behind him. He sighed as he answered the last question and gathered up his belongings. As he rose, he glanced behind him. All he could see was the top of Lana's head as she was hunched over her paper. He did see that she had made a little drawing at the corner of the test above her name. He did not look too closely for fear that the professor would think he was cheating. Jared nodded at the man as he dropped the paper on the professor's desk.

Jared hung out in the hallway for a few minutes, waiting for Lana to come out. When she did, she was with the tall guy who had spoken to her before the test. Jared scowled as he had forgotten about him.

"How did you do?" Lana stopped and asked Jared. The boy lingered behind her, staring daggers through Jared. "I think I did better than I thought I would. Those questions, though, I don't think most of them were even remotely connected to the textbook."

"It was tough." Jared could not think of anything to say about the test. He looked at the notebook Lana had clutched to her chest. "Hey, that drawing on there. That's what you wrote on your test paper above your name."

Lana turned the notebook over and looked at the back. She then gave Jared a strange look.

"Why were you looking at my test paper?"

"Yeah, why were you looking at her test paper, dude?" The tall guy titled his head and gave Jared a smug look.

"What? Are you her echo?" Jared was getting aggravated. He turned his attention back to Lana. She had a wide-eye look like she was amused. The corners of her mouth were twitching as if she was trying not to laugh. "I looked back at you when I got up to turn mine in. I was going to take yours for you, like a gentleman." Jared shot the other guy a look. "You were still working on it. I glanced down and saw that symbol. What does it mean?"

"Hey, Roger, we are getting a game together before biology. Want to shoot some hoops with us?" Another guy stopped and spoke to 'Roger.' The new tall guy appeared to be older and eyed Lana a little longer than Jared liked.

"Yeah, Roger, why don't you go shoot some hoops? Lana and I need to talk about something." Jared gave Roger a fake smile and proceeded to keep talking to Lana. "So, that symbol, what does it represent?"

Jared watched as Roger paused and looked at Lana. Then, without a word, he turned and followed the other guy. Jared thought perhaps he had won that round.

"You don't know what this is?" Lana pointed to the drawing on the back of her notebook. "Really?"

"Swirly lines. Pretty swirly lines."

"It's the infinity symbol." Lana rolled her eyes. "It really has to do with math and stuff. But, to me, it means beyond forever. As far as I can imagine, and then a whole lot more."

Jared watched the dreamy look pass into Lana's eyes. She had beautiful green eyes.

"So, why do you put it over your name?" Lana looked at her notebook and crinkled her brow. "It was over your name on your paper."

"That was more than just a glance, mister. Were you trying to see some of my super wrong answers?" Lana giggled. Her whole face lit up as if someone had set a spotlight on her.

"No, really, I just glanced—"

"I'm just kidding you. Don't take me seriously. I am all sass." Lana looked straight into Jared's eyes for a moment. He became mesmerized. "Do you have another class now?"

Jared snapped back to reality and looked at his watch.

"This is Tuesday, right?" He blushed with embarrassment. "I don't have another class until after lunch.

"Me neither. Have you had breakfast?"

"No, I never eat breakfast before this class. I barely roll out of bed." Jared smiled realizing that he probably looked like the morning bum that he was. His hand went to the stubble on his face. "I did brush my teeth and comb my hair."

"No worries. You don't see any makeup on this face or styled hair. I think I wore these clothes yesterday. This is our last chance to be bums before we have to be adults, right?"

"Exactly. I like the way you think, Lana—"

"Bouvier. I'm Lana Bouvier. And, you are?"

"Jared. Jared Kennedy."

"Oh, my goodness. My grandmother would have loved to witness this meeting. A Bouvier meets a Kennedy." Jared gave Lana a puzzled look. "Ever heard of Jackie Bouvier?"

Jared shook his head. "She married a man named John Kennedy."

"Oh, that Jackie. Yes, I've heard of her. Didn't realize that was her maiden name. Are you related to her?"

"Not that I am aware of. Then, again, aren't we all related?" Lana tilted her head and smiled at Jared. He remained silent as all he could think at that moment was that he did not want to be related to her. At least, not yet. "Anyway, do you want to go get some breakfast at the diner on Norwood Avenue?" Lana shifted the conversation.

Jared's mind raced as he wondered if Lana had just asked him out on a date. He watched her friendly smile change to a serious look.

"Yes. Love the diner. I'm starving. Let's go."

"If you don't want to go, it's not a big deal. I just thought that since you were standing out here that you wanted to talk. You may have other things to do now." Lana turned and began walking toward the doorway that led to the quad.

"No. I don't have anything to do. I'm sorry that I hesitated. That's a sure sign that my brain needs food. Please let me go with you." Jared rolled his eyes as he realized how pitiful and childlike he had sounded.

"Okay." Lana turned back toward him with a smile. "Have you eaten there before? I can't remember the name of the place. They have the most awesome ham and cheese omelet. It's huge!"

As they walked out into the quad area, the warmth of a

lingering summer hit their faces. Students were walking in all directions between classes. The activity created a hum in the atmosphere. Lana stopped for a moment to speak to a girl who walked up to them. As Jared hung back watching, it occurred to him that out of all of the thousands of students around him, he sat down in front of this particular girl in Economics class. Even his young inexperienced spirit knew that something had just occurred to him that was life changing.

"My friend Valerie asked if you were dating anyone." Lana leaned up and whispered in his ear as they walked on the sidewalk toward Norwood Avenue.

"She did. What did you tell her?"

"I said I had just met you. Well, I guess that isn't exactly right. You've sat in front of me for a couple of weeks now. That probably counts as meeting." Lana paused as they waited to cross the street. "So, what should I tell her? She seems quite interested."

Jared did not consider himself to be brave. Even though his good looks got him his fair share of attention, he was not a player like some of his friends. His dating had been limited, mostly because of his own insecurity in approaching girls. Something inside him said that it was not the time to be shy.

"Yes. I am dating someone." Jared held open the door of the diner. He watched as Lana's expression subtly changed. He thought she might be trying to not look disappointed by what he had said. After she passed through the doorway in front of him, he continued. "Tell her that I am dating a girl I met in one of my classes." His sudden jolt of bravery told him to pause for effect. "Her name is Lana and she likes infinity symbols."

"WE WERE BASICALLY inseparable after that." A tear ran down Jared's face. "You know, I'm going to tell you something that few people know. The police found Lana's Jeep a couple of weeks after she was taken. They tore it apart looking for evidence. All the DNA samples just led them right back to me and Lana." Jared paused and took a deep breath. "Eventually, they returned the Jeep to me. I never drove it again. It's sitting in the extra garage behind Dad's house. Every year on the anniversary of the night she was taken, I go there and sit inside of it for a while. I remember that night for everything it was. I'd like to say it is comforting. The truth is that it's my penance. I should have never gotten out of the vehicle that night."

"Jared, you couldn't have known what was going to happen. It was someone else's plan."

"Someone else's plan. That's right. Someone wanted to steal a beautiful life. We were just in the wrong place at the wrong time. Only we weren't. It was the twelfth anniversary of our first date and, up until that split second on the drive home, it had been one of my most wonderful memories. But Lana knew that something was wrong when we stopped. She sensed danger. She tried to stop me from getting out." Jared became lost in a tunnel of memories. It was only Karin's voice that brought him out again.

"What were you about to say? Something you never told anyone. Tell me. I'm here." Jared felt the warmth of Karin's hand on his arm.

"There was something that the police missed in the back of the Jeep. Or, at least, they never mentioned it to me. We kept a small bag in a compartment in the back. It was like a zippered bag you might have used to store your pencils in during school. I had a bag like that in both of our vehicles. It contained small things that you might need like pliers, electrical tape, a little extra money, and a black Sharpie. Lana knew it was there. The interior of the Jeep was a light grey. When the Jeep was returned to me, on the outside of the storage area where I kept that little bag, there was an infinity symbol drawn in black. I might have never seen it if the light hadn't been hitting just right. I combed the Jeep myself looking for more clues after that. I never found anything else. Just one last message from her to me. It was just like seeing her hand on the glass as the abductor drove away that night. She was trying to tell me something. I heard her, loud and clear."

"Oh, Jared. No wonder seeing that symbol is so heart-wrenching for you."

"It's not really seeing it. I obviously see it every day on this chain I have dangling here." Jared took hold of the large pendant that was hanging from his rearview mirror. He had found it in Lana's belongings shortly after she was taken. It was much larger than the one that she had worn around her neck. "It's seeing it on another person that brings up those dark feelings. I didn't want you to feel that our relationship was haunted by my past. It's taken me a long time to reach the point that I felt I could be with another person. I never thought there would be anyone besides Lana."

"I understand. I'm happy you found a place in your heart for me. I don't want you to ever feel like you cannot talk about Lana. Talking about her will keep her memory alive."

"That's the thing. That's the worst part. She could still be alive out there somewhere." Jared stretched out his hand in front of him, almost touching the windshield. In one swift motion, he then balled his hand into a fist and hit the dashboard. "All I want is to know that she is safe. If she is gone, I want to know that she went quickly with as little suffering as possible."

They were both silent for a while. Jared watched as several families pulled into the parking lot and unloaded items for a fun afternoon. It was everything that he had always imagined that he would do with Lana—a couple of children, a normal suburban life. 'Normal' was a term that referred to other people. Normal was something he envied.

Chapter Ten

"JARED, YOU JUST DO NOT KNOW HOW much we appreciate you driving the bus for us today." Mrs. Moody beamed as she stood next to the bus while the children, one by one, stepped on the bus. The bubbly blonde had the energy of a new teacher even though her years as the principal were over thirty. "Oh, and the discount that the company also gave us, just because it was for you. It's wonderful. Thank you so much."

Before Jared could respond, Mrs. Moody's smile turned to a stern look as she reprimanded a young boy for pushing one of his classmates. He looked up to see Karin and the rest of her class coming down the walkway. Karin was walking beside a thin girl with long strawberry blonde hair. To be going on a fun field trip, the girl looked quite sad.

A few minutes later, all the students were loaded on the bus. The chatter was deafening.

"Okay, students. Listen up!" Jared kept staring straight ahead as he heard Karin put her 'teacher voice' on. To be a petite, often soft-spoken, woman, she could belt out some loud orders to fifth graders. "You will have plenty of time to chat on the two-hour drive to the aquarium. Right now, you are going to listen to me." The noise continued. "OR, I will tell our driver to turn the bus off and open the door so you can all get off and go back to class and take a test."

Silence fell upon the land. From his rearview mirror, he could see Mrs. Moody a few rows back. She caught his eye and winked.

"That's better. We are very happy to have Mrs. Moody and Mrs. Kleene with us today. As your teachers and principal, we expect all of you to be on your best behavior. Our chaperones are Jerome's mother, Mrs. Watley, and Shane's father, Mr. Dexter. I expect all of you to show them the proper respect and listen to them as you would your own parents. There will be consequences if you do not. Last, but certainly not least, I would like to introduce you to our driver, Mr. Kennedy." Jared turned around in his seat and waved. "As I told you a couple of weeks ago as we were finishing our fundraising, because of Mr. Kennedy's and the bus company's generosity, we were able to afford for everyone in our class to go on this trip. We must be kind and considerate to Mr. Kennedy. If he gets on this microphone and tells you to do something, you must stop what you are doing and obey. This could be regarding our safety, so pay attention. Let's show him how grateful we are." Karin started clapping and everyone joined in with applause and cheers.

"Thanks, everyone." Jared took the microphone from Karin. "I'm happy to be your driver today. I have one important announcement. Is everyone listening closely?"

There was not a sound on the bus. Jared pushed the button on the CD player in the console. Immediately, Kool and the Gang could be heard singing their popular 1980s hit *Celebration*. The fact that the song came out before most of their parents learned how to drive did not seem to matter as the students began to sing and dance in their seats. Karin put her hand over her eyes and shook her head in disbelief. Jared looked up at his rearview mirror. He could see Mrs. Moody with a big smile on her face, seat dancing with the student next to her. It was going to be a good day.

DESPITE HER SEAT in the third row, the girl with the strawberry blonde hair was still sitting in her seat when all of the other children got off the bus. Jared could see the male chaperone, Mr. Dexter, waiting on the sidewalk to make sure everyone got inside safely.

"You're going to miss all the fun, young lady." Jared smiled at the child. "What's your name?"

"Hope." Her soft voice was barely over a whisper.

"Hi, Hope. It's nice to meet you." Jared leaned on the seat in front of her. "You heard Miss Tyler introduce me as Mr. Kennedy. But I'm really just Jared."

Jared recalled hearing Karin mention a girl named Hope on numerous occasions. She worried about the child's questionable home life.

The girl looked up at him with her big blue eyes. Jared felt a twinge of sadness as he wondered how anyone could hurt a child.

"Aren't you excited to get here?"

"The time will go by too fast. This is my way to slow it down."

Hope gave Jared a weak smile as she pulled her small backpack over her shoulders and walked past him and down the steps to the sidewalk. Jared felt a tug on his heart as he watched her catch up with the group at the aquarium's entrance. Karin was still holding the door open. She gave Hope a quick hug as they both walked inside.

"Thanks for volunteering to help our kids, Mr. Kennedy." Mr. Dexter was standing on the sidewalk as Jared locked the bus. "Some of these students would not have been able to pay their part. Your generosity made it possible for everyone to come. Even that quiet girl who was the last one off."

"She seems like a sweet child." Jared extended his hand to Mr. Dexter. "And the name is Jared. It is my pleasure to help."

"Great to meet you, Jared. I'm Mike Dexter." The two men shook hands. "Hope is a great kid. It's a shame she has to live in such a difficult situation."

"You know her family?"

"Sort of. We live in the same neighborhood. There's about a block between us. Hope was in school before my wife and I knew there was even a child in that house. You never see anyone outside unless they are getting into a vehicle. Even when her father mows his yard, he does it right at the edge of dark. It's a very strange situation."

"You think there is abuse going on?" Jared and Mike began slowly walking up the sidewalk to the entrance.

"We've had our suspicions. It is less about what we see and more about what we don't. We live in a nice neighborhood with strong working families. People are friendly with each other. Children play together. Neighbors know each other. As I mentioned, you don't see these people in their own yard, much less anyone else's. No smiling and waving if you do see the father out. No one ever remembers seeing the mother before she died. One of the neighbors finally called social services. We know that a social worker came and investigated. The only thing that changed was that the girl, who the neighbor had glimpsed through the window a few times, started going to school. It was Hope's kindergarten year. She's attended school regularly since. I don't think she ever misses a day."

"Hope seems timid." Jared paused and furrowed his brow. "That's not the right word."

"Hope is unemotional. She is quite smart and engaged. Yet, she rarely shows any feelings." Mike stopped on the sidewalk as they reached the entrance. "I work evening shift, so that gives me the opportunity to volunteer on a regular basis in my son's classes. I enjoy working with kids. I probably should have been a teacher myself. There are not that many fathers who have the opportunity to help the teachers. They like having a male influence around as some of the children live in single parent homes and don't see their fathers often."

"My hat's off to you for taking the time to be involved like that. Now that you mention it, I have heard Karin speak of you. She appreciates your involvement."

"I've observed Hope a lot over the last three years. Her intelligence is striking. She grasps concepts almost instantaneously. But she seems to be missing the emotion gene, for lack of a better term. My wife and I have tried to interact with her father and get him to allow Hope to play with Shane after school. He always refuses, makes some excuse. I wouldn't say he is rude to us, but it's become obvious that we are not welcome. The teachers make sure that the school nurse checks Hope for any signs of physical abuse. None are found. She seems to be cared for in all of the basic ways. Emotionally, I think she must live in darkness. It's as if someone took that away from her before she learned to miss it."

Jared pondered Mike's words as they followed the children around the aquarium. Most of the children had expressions of excitement as they saw all of the different species of aquatic creatures in their vibrant colors swimming with bursts of energy. Delighted squeals and the roar of chatter filled the building as the children moved from exhibit to exhibit. Jared searched for the same expressions on Hope's face. Just as Mike had said, it was void of emotion. She looked interested and carefully read all of the panels at each exhibit, lingering at the ones that seemed more docile. The aura of sadness that seemed to hover around her drew him. Standing from a distance, he realized that her expression mimicked the feelings he carried with him each day. As he continued to function as an adult, he could put on an expected smile for appearances. This child had not learned to conform to what society expected of her. No one had taught her to pretend.

Looking around, he realized that the other teachers and chaperones were moving on with the bulk of the children, Mike stood back a few feet from him watching Hope and a couple of boys who seemed keen on mischief. As the boys moved on toward the others, Mike caught Jared's eye.

"I'll stay with her."

Jared smiled as he answered Mike's unspoken question.

Mike nodded and followed the two boys. Jared watched as Mike walked between them to break up a shoving match that was going on. Jared returned his attention to Hope. While he had been watching Mike and the boys, Karin had slipped back around the corner and was talking to Hope. Jared smiled as he thought about how teachers might make great spies with their stealth-like abilities.

"You've stood here a long time, Hope. Do you have a question?"

Jared watched as Karin spoke to the child. He had previously noticed that Hope stayed at one display until the other children had left to go to the next one.

"No, Miss Tyler. I just want to be able to look at it by myself."

"I understand. We need to stay together as a group though."

"Miss Tyler, is it okay if I stay with Hope and look at the exhibit?" Jared's question caught Karin off guard. She tilted her head and looked at him questioningly. "You can really study each one carefully when you don't have to look over anyone's shoulder. You can hear the recorded message better when people aren't jabbering."

Hope turned around and looked up at Jared. For a split second, a smile crossed her face. She quickly caught herself and turned back toward the glass. As Jared looked from Hope to Karin, he saw that Karin's eyes were filled with tears. She quickly shook off the emotion and cleared her throat.

"That will be fine. Hope, I am counting on you to keep an eye on Mr. Kennedy. We don't want him to wander off and get lost."

Without turning back toward them, Hope shook her head affirmatively. Karin reached over and squeezed Jared's arm, mouthing a "thank you," before walking away to catch up with the others.

"Have you ever been to an aquarium before?" As they moved to the next exhibit, Jared began talking to Hope.

"No."

A few moments passed as they both intently looked at a group of penguins. Jared quickly counted almost two dozen in different portions of the large glassed area.

"I like their tuxedos." Jared watched as two of the larger penguins walked toward a small area of water. One of the penguins seemed to be trying to get away from the other for some reason. Jared smiled in amusement. As he turned to look at Hope, he found her staring at him with a puzzled look on her face.

"Tuxedos?"

"Yes, you know all those shiny black and white feathers make them look like they are wearing tuxedos."

Hope did not seem to be buying Jared's statement as she turned back to watch the penguins.

"I wonder why they are on display at an aquarium." Jared kept talking. Hope gave him another look. "Penguins aren't fish. They are birds."

"Yes, but they can swim. They don't fly. They are aquatic birds."

"Oh, I see." Jared smiled to himself. "It looks like it must be time for lunch. Everyone is heading to the restaurant." Jared leaned down to Hope and whispered as they walked toward the restaurant. "I really hope they don't serve fish. That would just be too much to have to eat fish in an aquarium."

Jared hoped that his comment would cause some sort of reaction from Hope. He never imagined that it would initiate a burst of emotion that would linger for quite a long time afterward. Hope turned to Jared and began to laugh. It started as a giggle, but only seconds passed before it was a full blown belly laugh. As they walked toward the rest of the group, her laugh grew louder. Everyone turned and looked at them as they made their way to the end of the serving line. The entire group, adults and children, stood in shock as Hope laughed so hard that she doubled over.

Jared thought it was the most beautiful sound he had ever heard.

"I WOULD NEVER have believed it if I hadn't heard it for myself."

Jared had sat with Hope as the two of them ate

their chicken tenders and French fries. He had watched curiously as the little girl had chosen mustard as one of her condiments. Jared laughed to himself as Hope dipped a fry into the mustard and took a big bite.

"What's so funny, Mr. Kennedy?"

Jared had forgotten that Mrs. Moody was sitting on the other side of him.

"Hope likes mustard with her fries." Hope looked up at Jared, stopping in mid-bite as he spoke. "It's a rare and an acquired taste. I acquired it when I was five. My Uncle Vic introduced me to it." Jared reached over and stuck one of his fries into Hope's mustard. Her eyes got big as she watched him. A little stray giggle left over from her recent outburst tried to escape. Jared caught Karin watching from the far end of the table as he put the fry in his mouth. Her smile was broad and understanding. Once again, he was glad that his father had exercised his matchmaking skills.

An hour later after everyone was fed, the children were given a few minutes in the aquarium's gift shop. Jared used the time to retrieve the bus from the parking lot and move it back to the front of the building. Jared watched as children and adults filed out to the sidewalk. Neither seemed to have the same level of energy they displayed when they arrived.

As the teachers and chaperones watched the tired students climb onto the bus, Jared listened as Karin whispered to Mrs. Moody.

"No one has ever heard her laugh before. She barely even smiles when something funny is said."

"I know; it was amazing. This wonderful man got her to laugh."

"What did you say to her, Mr. Kennedy?"

Mrs. Moody gave him a questioning look. It reminded him of one exceptionally tough elementary school teacher he had.

"We were catching up with the group as you were going into the restaurant and I told her that I hoped we didn't have to eat fish."

"Oh, my. That wasn't even a good joke." Mrs. Moody's blunt comment took Jared by surprise.

"Well, I guess you had to be there." Jared rolled his eyes. "She didn't like my comment about penguins wearing tuxedos either."

"I'm sure not. Hope takes things very literally. She doesn't seem to understand sarcasm."

While Hope had been the last one off the bus, she was the first one to get back on. As Jared climbed on and stood by his seat, he looked around to see where she was seated. This time, she had taken the window seat in the first row on the right side. It was the seat right next to Karin.

"Did everyone have a good time?"

Despite the tired looks on the children's face, they gave him an excited roar and began chatting loudly among themselves. Jared thought he saw a brief look of happiness cross Hope's face. It was almost undetectable it passed so quickly, as her face returned to the expressionless state that appeared to be her normal.

"THEY WERE REALLY A great group of children. I guess that is a credit to their teachers." Jared gave Karin a wink as they opened the menus before them. After they returned from the trip, Karin insisted on taking Jared out to dinner. "It was a good day."

"I suppose that teachers should not compare students. You are right though; this group of kids is exceptional. That can mostly be attributed to their parents."

"What about Hope's parents? I think I remember hearing you speak of her before. I don't remember her story. Mike Dexter mentioned that they have witnessed some strange behavior from her father."

"Oh, yes. Hope. That sweet child has given me more sleepless nights than I can count. I worry about her. Hope lives with her father. He's a strange man. It's hard to put into words. He seems to exercise great control over Hope, even when he is not in the room. Her previous teachers say the same thing. Mrs. Moody despises him. He intermittently interacts with administration or faculty and he refuses to do more, even when direct requests are made to him."

Jared watched as Karin swirled her straw around in her glass of iced water. It was an unconscious habit he noticed she did when she was deep in thought.

"What has your interaction with him been like?"

"I've only met him once. It was last year when Hope was in Mrs. Dimarrio's class. Hope became very sick during class. She had a stomach bug and was vomiting. It was time for the children to go out for recess, so I stayed with Hope while we waited for her father to arrive. As you can imagine, Mrs. Dimarrio could handle two classes of children on a playground much better than I could." Karin took a sip of her water and smiled. "Anyway, Hope's father came. He was not rude in any way but wasn't friendly. I didn't like how firmly he gripped Hope's arm as he led her out of the room. He didn't seem to fill the role of a caring father."

"That's a shame. Mike told me about how intelligent she seems. She wasn't talkative during our short time together, but I could see a little bit of an interesting personality I think she is holding back."

"I get the impression that, aside from school, she spends a lot of her time alone. I think this is one of the reasons she has not developed as much emotionally. In intelligence, she is ten years old. Emotionally, she is younger. Even when her father is not around, he's still in control. It's like he is in her head."

"And her mother is deceased?"

"Yes, as I understand it, she died before Hope started school."

"Mike says that his neighbors have wondered about abuse in the home. Was there anything suspicious related to her death?"

"I have no idea." Karin paused and started twirling her straw again. Her expression changed from wonder to worry. "I might need to ask Mrs. Moody what she remembers about when Hope first started school. I do not recall there ever being any issues with Hope being uncared for. She always is clean and her clothes are in good shape. She doesn't appear malnourished."

"No siblings, I presume."

"None that I am aware of. From what we know from the neighbors, like Mike Dexter, if it wasn't for her going to school, I wonder if anyone would know that she existed."

"That's a bold statement." Jared was surprised at Karin's bluntness.

"I was not exaggerating when I said that I have lost sleep worrying about this child. When you watch a child show such little emotion day after day, you have to wonder why she has built up such a shell." Jared saw tears forming in Karin's eyes. He reached across the table for her hand. "As teachers, we try to maintain a caring distance from our students. We cannot get too involved in their lives. In my ten years of teaching, I've never before felt so compelled to want to get a child out of a situation. Mrs. Dimarrio said something similar to me one day in the teachers' lounge. She said she knew that Hope would haunt her dreams in her retirement."

"At least Hope has people who care about her at school. You can offer her love and the security of your confidence.

Perhaps, if she receives that throughout the rest of her childhood, it will be enough to help her overcome this in adulthood."

"In another year, she will not have the safety net of Meadows Elementary to nurture her. It's harder for middle school teachers to spend that much time. The kids change classes and are not with just one teacher all day. We really hoped that social services would find some evidence to remove Hope from that house."

"There's no assurance that she would go into a better situation though."

"No, but at least she would be away from whatever has made her so hollow. Oh, I hate to use that word. I do not think that is who she really is. She needs love."

"Maybe you should try getting her involved in some after school activity that would give her more time away from home and in the company of others. Even, if it was just with you."

"Jared, I thought that I was attracted to you because you are so handsome. It's because you are brilliant. That is a wonderful idea."

"Brilliant. Not sure that is an accurate description. Hungry is though. Where is our pizza?"

Chapter Eleven

"**W**ELL? IS HOPE'S FATHER GOING TO allow her to work on your project after school?"

Jared watched as Karin took a steaming casserole dish out of her oven. Jared was amazed at the meals Karin prepared after a long school day. He knew that Mrs. Moody was planning to try to contact Hope's father to see if he would allow Hope to stay after school to help Karin with a project.

"She said that at first he was hesitant. But when she explained that I would drop Hope off each evening, he seemed to soften."

"Does Hope normally go home on the bus?"

"Yes. I guess he didn't want to worry about how she would get home."

"From what you have said, I wonder if 'worry' is an accurate word."

"Probably not, it is more likely that he did not want to be inconvenienced."

"Does Hope know about this yet?"

"Yes, Mrs. Moody told her as Hope was waiting to catch the bus. She said that Hope seemed concerned that her father would not like it."

"Children shouldn't be afraid of their parents."

"Your parents never made you feel afraid? My mother could give me a look that stopped me in my tracks."

"I'm not referring to being afraid to disappoint or get into trouble. From what you have told me, it seems that Hope has a real fear of her father. Like a fear of what will happen if he is not happy with something. From my limited interaction with her, she seems to have developed a shell to try to protect herself."

"She has. That's the main reason why I want her to spend some afternoons with me. I want her to have some positive one-on-one interactions. I think she may need to have more female interaction, since her mother is gone." Karin placed the casserole dish on the table.

"I'm sure you are right. I know it is none of our business. But aren't you curious as to what happened to the mother?" Jared waited for Karin to bring a bowl of salad before they both sat down.

"I'm beyond curious. After what I have heard from Mike

Dexter and his wife, it makes me wonder if it shouldn't be an episode of one of those news program investigations. No one in their neighborhood ever remembers seeing Hope's mother. No one."

"So, Hope is the only evidence that she existed."

"Exactly."

"I'm not sure there is much that can be done if no one has reported anything criminal."

"Yes. The neighbors tried by calling in social services. There must not have been any visible signs of abuse." Karin paused as Jared began helping himself to the food. "I only want to do everything I can to make a difference in this young girl's life. Maybe my time with her will reveal something I can do to help make her life better."

As they began to eat, Jared thought about what Karin had said. He wondered if what happened to Lana might have been prevented by the act of someone getting involved. Maybe if someone had revealed suspicions about the behavior of Lana's abductor, he could have been stopped.

"Karin, do you remember meeting Beth and her family?"

"Yes, she is the detective who worked on Lana's case, right?"

"Yes, over the years, I became friends with Beth and her husband. She still plays a role in keeping Lana's case alive. What would you think about maybe talking to her about Hope?"

"Oh, Jared, I don't know. That sort of thing goes beyond my authority as a teacher."

"Okay, let me rephrase that. What would you think about me talking to her about Hope?" Jared smiled as he took a bite of his salad. When Karin did not immediately respond, Jared continued. "What if I asked Mrs. Moody if it was okay?"

"Well, she is still singing your praises about making Hope laugh."

"I am sure that Beth can be very discreet. If nothing else, maybe it will reveal something about the family as a whole which might prove beneficial in your interaction with Hope."

Karin reached across the table and took Jared's hand.

"You are such a good man. It makes me sad that you have had such heartache in your life."

"It makes me grateful that you are patiently understanding of that. I have been one lucky man to have had two wonderful women in my life."

"Including Mrs. Dimarrio." Karin released Jared's hand and resumed eating. "I saw you two making eyes at each other when you came to pick me up the other day."

"You should just be thankful that there is still a Mr. Dimarrio." Jared winked as he reached for another roll.

"Talk to Mrs. Moody. I think she will approve of involving Beth in a quiet manner. I believe that the school psychologist will approve as well."

"We will find a way to help Hope. Even if it means that Mike Dexter and I have to pay her father a visit."

"Jared." Karin's voice changed on a dime to her teacher tone.

"A friendly neighborly one."

"WHAT A WONDERFUL surprise!' Karin gave Jared a huge smile as he walked into her classroom. "To what do Hope and I owe this pleasure?"

Jared watched as Hope looked toward him. Her expression was more curious than happy. It had been two weeks since the girl began helping Karin in the afternoons.

"You mentioned last night that you and Hope were going to finish up your first project today. I thought that called for a celebration. So I took off early and stopped at the ice cream parlor. I took a chance that perhaps you both liked banana splits."

"I don't think I have ever had one." Hope's voice was monotone.

"What?" Both Jared and Karin spoke with surprised looks on their faces.

"I've read about them. I've had the parts separately."

"Parts separately?" Jared made eye contact with Karin as he questioned Hope.

"I've eaten bananas and I've eaten ice cream. I've never eaten them together. Is it good?"

"You are about to find out."

Jared had not spared any expense when he stopped to purchase the desserts. The owner of the ice cream parlor was a retired police officer who Jared had met when Lana disappeared. The man always had a listening ear for Jared during those first few months. When he retired about a year later, Jared began making weekly visits to his business.

"Jared, I have never seen such huge banana splits." Karin's eyes grew large as she opened up the container and placed one in front of Hope. "Is that three different scoops of ice cream?"

It was Hope's eyes that Jared concentrated on. Despite the stoic expression she kept most of the time, he could see wonder and excitement growing behind the little eyes. He had not noticed before what a beautiful color they were.

"Yes, there's chocolate, strawberry, and banana. Vanilla is just too plain for a banana split from Captain Sweets' parlor."

"Oh, Captain Sweets,' I have heard that it is wonderful." Karin handed Hope a couple of napkins. "Let's be careful not to get any on your clothes."

As Jared and Karin sat down on each side of Hope and opened their containers, they watched as the young girl carefully put her spoon into the dessert and came out with a small bite of banana with some of the chocolate ice cream and syrup. Jared held his breath as the spoon went into Hope's mouth and she consumed the first bite. She closed her eyes as a small smile crossed her face. Jared looked at Karin; she was watching Hope intently. They locked eyes and Jared winked.

"Well, Hope, I think I am just going to have to show you how to properly eat a banana split. You are doing it wrong."

Jared felt a tinge of sadness as he saw how quickly the smile left Hope's face as she set her spoon down. He would quickly make it right. Jared stabbed his spoon into the middle of his banana split and got a huge bite with two of the ice cream flavors, a big chunk of banana, syrup and whipped cream. In one seamless move, he took that spoon straight into his mouth, syrup and whipped cream around his mouth was all that remained. He looked like he had a white moustache. What happened next was more than he hoped for when he stopped to get the treats. Hope laughed. It started in her belly and worked up to her mouth and became a full-fledged little girl laugh.

"You are so funny, Mr. Kennedy."

Jared glanced at Karin. Her eyes were filled with tears. For a moment, they connected. He knew that neither could hold the gaze for long or they would both be crying.

Jared took another big messy bite. This time, Karin did the same. She had whipped cream on her nose. Hope laughed even harder. Then she mimicked them taking a huge bite of her own. With the agility and speed that Jared could only assume came from being a teacher of young children, Karin quickly grabbed a small towel off of a nearby table and wrapped it around the front of Hope just before a dollop of chocolate ice cream landed on her chest.

Hope looked down at the towel and up at Karin. A thankful look was on her face. They knew the words she did not speak. Hope was relieved that she would not have to explain an ice cream stain when she returned home.

Once they had each eaten as much of the desserts as they could hold, Karin picked up the leftovers and straightened up the rest of the room. Jared and Hope remained at the small table in a sugar stupor. After a few moments of silence, Jared noticed that Hope looked up at the clock and her little forehead crinkled with what appeared to be worry. Her hand reached for a necklace that had been hiding under her shirt. She moved it around her neck and let the pendant rest in view. The sight of it took his breath causing him to make a gulping noise. Hope gave him a concerned look.

"That's an unusual necklace you have on. Where did you get it?"

"It was my mother's." The words slapped Jared in the face like a bucket of cold water. "It's the only thing I have of hers. Dad burned everything else."

Jared's heart began racing so fast that he was almost lightheaded. He had to focus. He couldn't let her see the emotion he was feeling. It would scare her.

"Burned everything? That's a shame. It certainly is a unique shape."

"It's an infinity symbol." Hope took hold of the pendant and looked down at it. "Not many people recognize it."

"No, you don't see infinity symbols very often."

Hope tugged on the symbol as she looked at it.

"That's not the most unusual part." Hope's voice turned to a whisper. "There's something else at the clasp."

The room began to spin as she spoke. Jared grabbed hold of the side of the chair. If he did not calm himself, he was certain he would go into cardiac arrest. Even a healthy heart could only stand so much shock.

"Are you okay?" Hope's soft voice made him focus. "You look a little sick."

"You know, I think I ate some bad Mexican food for lunch. Convenience store burritos are a bad idea." Jared let out a nervous chuckle. His answer seemed to appease Hope. "What's different about it? Can I see?"

Hope reached behind her head for the clasp. What was certainly only a couple of seconds seemed like forever to Jared. As he watched her small hands unclasp the necklace and then pull it down in front of her, Jared's mind raced back to when he first saw the necklace he gave Lana. She had doodled the infinity symbol so many times during their freshman year of college, that he could not imagine getting her something as boring as a heart on their first Valentine's Day together. The jeweler at the store had been a kind gentleman who spoke of his first love who had been his wife for over forty years. The man had told Jared that as unusual as the necklace was, they needed to add something else to it that would make it an even more special token of their love. So the jeweler had added the extra little charm that dangled from the clasp, making it the perfect present for Lana.

"Mr. Kennedy, are you okay?"

Jared had drifted so far into the past that he had lost what was going on in the present. His eyes met Hope's. They were filled with concern.

"I'm just fine—"

His voice left him as he looked down at the necklace she had carefully placed on the table between then. On the right side of the open clasp was a tiny star. The same star he told Lana he would pull down from heaven if she wanted. Jared's hand began to shake as his fingers reached for the necklace. He could feel all the blood leaving his head.

"Mr. Kennedy, you are scaring me. I'm going to get Ms. Tyler. You must be really sick. You don't look so good."

It might have been the expression on her face as her forehead furrowed in concern. It could have been the lightness of her step as she ran out of the room. It could have been a million little things or nothing at all. It was everything and nothing. Yet, a familiar and distant voice spoke to him. A voice that filled his heart with love and pain. The voice said, "This is my daughter."

"Jared, are you okay?" Karin came running back into the classroom with Hope on her heels.

"Ah, yeah, I'm okay. I just felt a little sick. I guess I forgot that my stomach isn't as young as it used to be." Jared laughed nervously. Karin furrowed her brow and started to speak as Jared held up his hand. "Isn't it time for you to take Hope home?"

Karin looked up at the clock above the blackboard. She quickly began helping Hope collect her things.

"If we leave right now, I think I can make it without being late." Karin glanced at Hope. Jared watched as the two looked at each other seriously. "We wouldn't want to cause your father to worry. Maybe I should call him and say we are on our way." Hope shook her head. "Jared, are you sure you are okay?"

"I'm fine. You take care of this young lady." Jared smiled at Hope as he handed her the necklace. He watched as she quickly, but carefully, put it back around her neck. As the child looked up at him, he searched her face for similarities to Lana's. He did not know if it was his mind trying to protect him or that the child did not bear more resemblance than Lana's coloring. "I hope that you liked the banana split." A small beginning of a smile returned to the child's face. She shook her head affirmatively as she turned to follow Karin.

"See you at my house later, okay?" Karin waved to Jared as she opened the door for Hope. He nodded and smiled before she closed the door behind them.

Jared stood up. His legs were shaky. His whole body was shaking. He walked over to the classroom window that faced the parking lot where the teachers parked. As he watched Karin and Hope hurriedly walk across the lot and get into Karin's car, a thousand thoughts raced through Jared's mind.

"There could be several reasons why that little girl has Lana's necklace." Jared began talking out loud to himself. "It could be that her mother was in on Lana's abduction. Or the abductor could have taken the necklace from Lana and given it to someone. Maybe the abductor pawned it and someone bought it later."

Despite all of the arguments he was making with himself, he knew without a doubt that they were only excuses for what he knew in the core of his soul to be true. He was drawn to Hope from the moment he saw her. It was not just that she was a poor little girl who needed a friend. His heart sensed that he had met the junior version of his true love. His heart knew it before his mind could ever process the truth.

"I'll save her, Lana." Jared spoke as he watched Karin's car move out of sight. "I cannot let my mind think about how she became yours. But, if this is your child, I will do whatever it takes to get her away from the life that you never would have willingly left her in. I will save your daughter. No matter what it takes or how long. I will not rest until she is safe from harm."

Chapter Twelve

"SIT DOWN, JARED. YOU'RE NOT making any sense. Start again and tell me slowly."

It had taken Jared almost an hour to drive to Beth Rivers' home. After trying to call her office, he was told that Beth had left for the day. Calls to her cell phone had gone straight to voicemail. Jared did the only other thing he knew to do. He drove straight there and sat parked on the street waiting. Her expression of surprise when she pulled into her driveway, quickly turning to concern as, even from a distance, her detective skills seemed to pick up on Jared's exasperated state.

"I've found Lana's daughter."

"That's what I thought you said before. I don't understand what you mean." Beth had ushered Jared into their kitchen area where she immediately began making coffee. "Why do you think it is Lana's daughter?"

"There's a little girl in Karin's class. Her name is Hope. She has Lana's necklace."

"Jared, there could be many necklaces that looked like the one Lana owned. I don't recall you telling me that it was engraved."

"No, it wasn't engraved, but it still had something unique about it. On our first Valentine's Day together, I gave her a necklace with an infinity symbol pendant."

"I remember the significance of the symbol. You have told us repeatedly that she never took the necklace off. I don't understand why you are so sure that this little girl has the necklace that belonged to Lana."

"The jeweler put something special on the clasp for me. It was a little star."

Jared sat down on the stool at the bar that separated the kitchen from the dining area. He looked at his hands. They were trembling. Taking a deep breath, he began to tell Beth the story.

"I believe I have told you that Lana and I met during our freshman year. We had only been in college a few weeks. Right before the semester ended in December, the week before exams, Lana got really sick. It was a very bad case of the flu. It was so bad that her roommates went and stayed in other rooms as they were afraid of catching what she had and being too sick to complete their classes.

This was before her father retired from the military, and he was on assignment somewhere far off on a long mission so he could not come home and see Lana during her holiday break between semesters. I was the only person she had to take care of her so that is what I did. I got permission from the person in charge of the dorm, and I moved in for a week and cared for her. Gradually, she got better and was able to take her exams and finish classes."

"You were an unusual young man. I imagine that by the flu you mean she was sick in many different ways."

"Oh, yes. Stuff was coming out of her every way it could. She was a mess and became quite weak after the first few days. I would carry her to the toilet and carry her to the bathtub. Before she and I were ever intimate, we were intimate in ways that many aren't even after they are married." Jared shook his head and smiled. "My mother was a nurse. She always had this 'do what it takes' attitude. I guess that is where I got that from. That, and the fact that I already loved Lana. I had to take care of her."

"So, what does this story have to do with the necklace?" Beth handed Jared a cup of coffee.

"Except when I went out to my classes or to get some food or medicine, we stayed in Lana's room the whole time. After a few days, when she began to feel better, we started watching old movies on one of the cable channels. Since we were getting close to the holidays, one of the movies on was *A Wonderful Life*. Lana was a big James Stewart fan."

"What girl isn't?" Beth smiled as she sat down across from Jared with her own cup of coffee.

"I had never seen the movie up until that point. There's the scene early on when James Stewart's character, George Bailey, tells his girlfriend, Mary, that if she wants the moon he will throw a lasso around it and pull it down for her. I told Lana I would do the same. Immediately, even in her sick and medicated state, she said that she would much prefer a star."

"So a star is on the clasp of the pendant?"

"Exactly. That pendant now hangs around the neck of a little strawberry blonde haired girl named Hope. She lives with a father who controls her even when he is not around. She shows little emotion. It's almost like she doesn't know how."

"And this girl's mother?"

"As far as we know, she died before Hope entered school."

"You know that I can't just randomly start investigating someone without evidence of a crime having been committed."

"Yes, I know. The neighbors and school officials have all been concerned about Hope's wellbeing."

"What have they done about those concerns?"

"I believe the neighbors alerted social services. I don't think they could find any evidence of abuse. I think this was after the mother supposedly died."

"Hope is a very pretty name." Karin delicately began the conversation. "I don't know any other little girls with that name. I wonder how your mother decided on that for you."

Jared sat quietly and watched as the child before him scrunched her forehead and thought. She tilted her head slightly as she did so.

"My mother told me that she named me Hope so that I would always remember."

"Remember what?"

"Remember that there was always hope that life would be better one day."

Like a vice slowly being tightened, Jared could almost feel her little hand taking hold of his heart just like her mother had done those many years ago. He had to remain quiet and allow Karin to talk to Hope.

"What was your mother's name?"

"I called her Mommie."

"Yes, that would be the right thing for you to do. I'm sure she loved hearing you say that." Karin darted her eyes at Jared. He could tell that she was seeing the tension that he was feeling. "What did other people call her? What was her first name?"

"I don't know."

Hope lowered her head. Her slumped shoulders and the

tight way she held her arms next to her body made her look even smaller than she was.

"What did your father call her?" Karin's voice was light and conversational.

"You."

"'You?' He called her 'You?'"

"Yes. He would say, '*You* get my dinner ready.' '*You* put that girl to bed.'"

It had been many years since Jared had allowed the all-consuming rage that was now filling every crevice of his being to emerge. It had taken years of therapy and a lot of driving miles for him to shake the feeling of always wanting to hit something in frustration. He was not a man of violence by nature. Yet, in the months after Lana was abducted, he had broken numerous baseball bats, a few windows, and had learned the art of patching sheetrock as he tried to deal with the frustrating feeling of helplessness and the sheer anger that the love of his life had been taken from him, right before his eyes.

As he consciously tried to calm himself so that his internal rage would not manifest itself for Karin and Hope to see, he tried to focus on why they were doing this. If Lana was Hope's mother, it seemed fairly certain that she was deceased. He might never know what really happened to her. This was his chance to help justice be carried out. He had to maintain control so that he could gather the evidence needed to get this child away from the evil that took Lana.

Jared had to make sure that the man was apprehended and imprisoned. As much as it sickened him to think about how this sweet little girl came into existence, Jared had no doubt that she was Lana's daughter. Once the realization had fully hit him on the day of the banana splits, he then saw Lana in every expression and movement the child made. He had no doubt.

"You don't know what her first name was? Like my first name is Karin and your first name is Hope."

"I don't think so. Is that bad?"

"No, Hope, it's not bad. I understand. You were very young when she died. You were too young to remember."

"I was not very young. I wasn't like a baby or anything."

"What do you mean?" Karin shifted her eyes toward Jared as she continued to question Hope.

"She died when I was in kindergarten."

Hope looked from Karin to Jared. Her eyes welled with tears. They were both so shocked to see this level of emotion from the child that neither one of them moved. It proved to work to their advantage as the girl kept talking.

"I came home from school one day and couldn't find her anywhere I looked. I was really afraid, but I asked my father where she was. He told me she was in the basement. I went down there and she was lying at the bottom of the stairs. There was a big gash in her head. I couldn't make her wake up." Hope put her face in her hands.

"Why don't you go to the restroom and get cleaned up

a little before I take you home? You don't want your father to ask why you have been crying, do you?"

Hope immediately stood up and shook her head negatively. Her whole demeanor changed in an instant. She was back to being the emotionless child. After she left the room, Jared spoke.

"Why in the world did you stop her from telling us about what happened to Lana?"

"Because you were sitting there looking like a pressure cooker that was ready to explode. You can't let Hope see you that way. She will get suspicious, or worse, scared of you."

"But we have got to get as much information as possible in order for the police to be able to get a warrant."

"And we will. But, if you tip her off, she will get scared. Her father is horrendous, but he is the only family she has."

"Only family she has. Oh, that just makes me sick. I had almost given up on ever finding Lana. I never imagined in a million years that there could possibly be a miniature version of her out there."

Karin shushed Jared as Hope crossed the doorway into the classroom. Jared turned and saw her walking toward him and was awestruck at the memory that surfaced from long ago.

"HEY, SLEEPYHEAD. I'VE been waiting downstairs for you for ten minutes. We are going to be late to class. You know that Mr. Yates docks us two points if we are late."

Jared had knocked before entering Lana's dorm suite. He knew though that it was likely that her other three suitemates were already in class. They were all biology majors and had early morning labs. Lana was the one who could always sleep in as her first class on Wednesdays was not until nine.

Lana's body and head was covered with her comforter. Jared could see her body jerking and heard a slight noise that he assumed was a laugh.

"You can play around all you want to. I am going to class." Jared turned to leave, thinking that he would call her bluff.

"Pyewacket is dead." Lana sobbed as she came out from under the comforter. Jared turned and saw that she was crying and had been for quite some time by the looks of her swollen face.

"Pie what?" Jared sat down on her bed and put his arm around her.

"Pyewacket. She's my cat." Lana started crying even harder. "She was my cat."

"I didn't even know you had a cat. I didn't think that cats were allowed in the dorms."

Lana stopped crying long enough to roll her eyes and shake her head.

"She lives at home with my Dad." The tears returned. "She lived at home. Pyewacket is gone now. Dad has already buried her in the back yard. I'll never see her again."

"I'm sorry, honey. That is very sad. But there'll be other cats. The world is full of cats."

From the instantaneous look on Lana's face, Jared knew he would regret those words.

"There will never be another Pyewacket. She was a Siamese just like in the movie."

"Movie? What movie? You've lost me."

"There was a movie called *Bell, Book, and Candle*. It starred James Stewart and Kim Novak. Kim Novak was a witch and she had a Siamese cat named Pyewacket. I watched the movie with my mother when I was little. She loved James Stewart, and Mom looked a lot like Kim Novak. The day after we watched the movie, we went to a pet store and got Pyewacket. A few months later, Mom was in the car accident. It was the last thing she gave me. She was my link to my Mom. And she's gone! They are both gone." Lana turned back toward her bed and buried her head in the pillows.

"I'm sorry. It's horrible. But Lana, honey, Mr. Yates said he might give a pop quiz today and he is giving out the information for how he wants our research paper to be written."

Lana sat up in the bed like a magnet had pulled her up. Without saying another word, she ran into the bathroom.

Jared could hear the water running in the sink, the sound of her electric toothbrush, and the toilet flushing, simultaneously.

"You want me to go on to class and tell Mr. Yates that you've had a family emergency."

Lana came out of the bathroom long enough to shake her head as she continued to brush her teeth.

"Okay, babe. Don't forget to get dressed."

Jared flew out of the building and made a hard run across the quad. Luckily, the building the class was in was one of the closest to Lana's dorm. By allowing his long legs to take three stairs at time, he barely made it into the classroom before the clock chimed nine. Mr. Yates gave him a look as he approached the desk.

"I'm sorry, Mr. Yates. I was with Lana. She is on her way. She's had a family emergency."

"Somebody better have died." Mr. Yates gruff voice belted out the words as he adjusted the glasses on his face.

"Someone did."

Jared replied, as he took his seat. His words caused a look of surprise to cross Mr. Yates' face. It quickly changed as he put a slide on the overhead projector and handed a stack of papers to one of the girls in the front row to hand out. The professor was beginning to talk about their term project, a research paper that would be worth fifty percent of the overall semester grade. Mr. Yates was notorious for just changing the assignment enough each semester that no one could either try to do it ahead of time or to submit a 'rerun,' as he called it, of another student's paper from previous years.

Mr. Yates was just about to begin discussing the outline of the paper when Lana appeared in the doorway. All eyes moved in her direction. Only one word could be used to describe her—pitiful. Her normally neat appearance was replaced by a disheveled look. Her clothes were wrinkled, as if they had been slept in. Her long hair was pulled back in a messy ponytail. Her face was swollen, red, and puffy, without even a tinge of makeup. Lana indeed looked like someone had died.

"Miss Bouvier, you are late. I understand that you claim you have had a family emergency. Who died?"

The classroom erupted in laughter. Lana shot a cold look at her audience.

"My cat. She was the last gift my mother gave me before she died in a car accident when I was eight."

Silence filled the room. A pin drop would have made a loud clatter. Jared glanced around to see the shocked looks of their classmates. Most now seemed interested in whatever was on their desks.

"Well, young lady, that is quite unfortunate." Mr. Yates' tone was a little less gruff, but still questioning. "What was your feline's name?" Jared surmised that the man was trying to trip Lana up. If she stumbled, it would be a sign of untruth.

"Pyewacket. This is a picture of her. Isn't she beautiful?" A sob escaped Lana's throat as she revealed the framed photograph she was carrying with her books. "Oh, she isn't beautiful anymore. My father has already buried her."

"Oh, there, there, dear." Mr. Yates' walked Lana to her desk with his hand on her arm. "Yes, she was a beauty. A name from a wonderful movie."

Lana sniffled and nodded as she sat down in her seat in front of Jared.

"My Mom and I loved the movie."

"Indeed. A James Stewart classic." Mr. Yates went back to the front of the class and adjusted the slide on the overhead projector. "Your research project will consist of three parts."

No more was said regarding Lana being late. Mr. Yates did not give a pop quiz. Fellow students came up and hugged her as she left class later. Lana was a pitiful girl.

Chapter Thirteen

"How in the world are we going to be able to get some of Lana's DNA?" Jared paced the floor of Beth Rivers' office. "You've said that you can't issue a search warrant unless we can get some evidence to link this child to Lana. She's been gone so long. Where could we possibly get her DNA?"

"What about a family member?"

"There are no family members. Lana had very few to start with and several of them have died since she disappeared. It would be a struggle to even find a cousin. I don't remember any of their last names. She had little contact with them while I knew her. A cousin seems quite removed when you are looking at something like DNA." Jared watched as it appeared that Beth remembered something. She went to a tall filing cabinet and began digging through files. "What is it? What are you looking for?"

"When Lana was just abducted, we used hair samples that we obtained from your apartment and matched them with a sample that we got from Lana's doctor."

"I remember that. It was how you tested the DNA in the Jeep to eliminate Lana and me from the other samples."

"It was one of the few aspects we got lucky with during those early days of the investigation. If I remember correctly, Lana had just visited her gynecologist the day before she was abducted. She had some tests done, including bloodwork. Their lab still had the vials of blood."

"How will that help us? Those vials must be long gone by now."

"We did an entire DNA workup on Lana. We wanted to make sure that we had a good concrete sample to compare to in the event—"

"I know, Beth. I can take it. In the event that you found any remains."

"Yes. It would have helped to provide closure for you as well as the prosecution of the case. What I will need to do is go back through the files and find that complete workup. It's possible that there are even still usable samples that could undergo more advanced screening. We should have enough information regarding Lana's genetic profile in order to connect her with a child, if she had one. Now, we just have to figure out a way to get a sample of this little girl's DNA. It's not likely that we will be able to get the father to willingly agree to such a test. If there was only a way to get a verifiable sample without getting permission, we—"

"Oh, Captain Rivers, I believe I may be one step ahead of you."

"Take your seats everyone. We have a special guest today. Settle down. I would like to introduce you to Captain Beth Rivers. Captain Rivers is in charge of the detective unit of the state police. She is going to talk to you today about how they collect evidence."

Jared stood in the back of the room and held his breath. He was amazed that Beth was willing to come to the school on the ruse of giving a presentation to Hope's class. Despite his apprehension about what she would think of his idea, Beth agreed to it more readily than he imagined. He thought that she realized it might be one of the last ways to find Lana, even if Lana was already gone. Having the cooperation of Hope's teacher and principal made the process smoother than it would have been otherwise.

"How many of you have seen television shows or movies about police investigations?" Almost all of the students raised their hands, Jared noticed. All except Hope.

"Some of those shows do not give the exact procedures regarding how police investigate crime scenes, but there are some good examples within them of how we collect evidence. Does anyone understand what DNA is?" One little boy raised his hand. "Yes, what's your name?"

"Martin."

"So, what is DNA, Martin?"

"It's who you are on the inside."

"Okay. That's one way to look at it. Anyone else have an idea?" Another child raised her hand. "Tell me your name and your answer."

"Mariah. I think it tells you who your relatives are."

"That's a good answer, too. DNA is the material that carries all the information about how you will look and function. Each piece of information is carried on a different section of DNA. Those sections are called genes. Those genes relay the information about what color your eyes will be and if you will be short like your mother or tall like your father. There are many ways that we can collect DNA. You may have seen on television where someone will have the inside of their cheek swabbed with a tool that looks like a cotton swab. That is one way that a person's DNA can be determined. Another way is through a small fragment of a person's hair or by sampling their blood."

"What about fingerprints?" Martin raised his hand and spoke at the same time.

"Fingerprints can help identify if a person has been at

a certain place. If a person's fingerprints are not within our database though, we cannot match them and confirm the person's identity. Prints do not, however, link us to another person genetically." Beth walked down one of the aisles of desks and turned to face a television on the wall. "I am going to show you a video to help explain DNA more fully. After we view this, with the help of a volunteer, I am going to show you how simple and easy it can be to get a sample of DNA to test."

Beth joined Jared in the back of the classroom. Mrs. Moody had positioned a chair next to Hope and was talking to her and pointing to the screen as the short film was playing. It was hard for Jared to interpret what the principal was saying to the girl. Mike Dexter slipped into the classroom and stood next to Jared.

"Mike, this is Captain Beth Rivers, she is giving a presentation to the class today." The two shook hands and nodded.

"I'm sure the kids will learn a lot today. Thanks for taking an interest in Hope's situation."

Jared gave Mike a wide-eyed look.

"Mrs. Moody talked with Rachel and me about it yesterday. That's why I am here today."

Jared's expression still showed his confusion.

"Rachel is my wife, and she is the attorney for the school system. Mrs. Moody wanted to get her feedback before she allowed Captain Rivers to proceed with the test."

"I had no idea."

"Because I have been such a fixture in this school for many years, Shane is our third child to attend here, I am sometimes used to help investigate situations that the principal or teachers are concerned about. Hope has been high on that list for many years. We have extensive documentation regarding many instances that are borderline. Rachel says this is a situation that we are going to err on the side of seeking the good of the child's welfare. If it reveals nothing substantial, we will revert to this being what it most certainly is—a learning opportunity for the class with a hands-on demonstration."

"Did you know my connection to Lana?"

"Yes. Working on second shift all these years has made me a news hound. I was one of the people who volunteered to look for Lana. I walked a lot of miles through the woods looking for her. We will never forget her."

"I'm sorry. I didn't remember meeting you—"

"Hold on. No apologizing is necessary. You never met me. If you had, you were not in the frame of mind to remember anyone. I still want to help find Lana. Even if that means the worst ending."

"I think you may be my new best friend, man." Jared slapped Mike on the back.

"That would be an honor."

"Okay, class. Did you enjoy that movie about DNA?" Captain Rivers walked back up to the front of the room as she clicked the DVD off. "I think that gives a great overview in a way that even an old police detective like me can understand."

Jared watched as the children chatted among themselves for a moment. It did not take long for Beth's silence to cause them to be quiet as well. Mrs. Moody remained in the chair next to Hope. Jared saw her give a slight nod to Karin who stood near the right wall of the classroom.

"I'm going to ask if one of you would like to volunteer to be our test subject. Then, I will take you through a list that gives you an idea regarding the type of information that we find out from a DNA test." Captain Rivers paused and looked around. "Who would like to volunteer? Raise your hand."

Jared was surprised that none of the students were raising their hands. It was like they knew that Hope needed to be the one. He smiled to himself as he wondered if Lana was somehow influencing what was happening.

Jared held his breath. He watched as Mrs. Moody whispered into Hope's ear. Time seemed to stop as he watched the little girl whom he knew with certainty was the daughter of his beloved Lana.

"Come on, you can do it." Jared whispered under his breath. "Lana, give her a little strength. I couldn't save you. Help me save your daughter."

And just like that, Hope raised her hand.

"Wonderful. Yes, the young lady in the back next to Mrs. Moody. Please come up here."

Jared did not hear anything else that Beth said. He was overcome with the power of the moment. He watched as Hope sat in a chair in front of Beth. Karin joined her and held her hand as Beth took the swab and ran it on the inside of Hope's mouth.

"That didn't hurt at all, did it?" Beth handed Hope a small lollipop after completing the swabbing.

"It tickled a little."

Hope held the lollipop in her hand before she got up from the chair and began walking back to her seat. Just before she reached it, she stopped and looked right straight at Jared. He locked eyes with her and froze. It almost felt like he was transcending time. As Hope gave him a small smile, he saw the face of Lana; he could not conceal the tears that pooled in his eyes. He was thankful when Mrs. Moody broke their gaze as she motioned to Hope to sit back down.

"You're okay, man. Sit down."

Mike's words brought Jared back to the present. He wiped his eyes and shook his head. He sunk into the chair that Mike had placed behind him. Jared felt as if a heavy weight had been lifted from his shoulders. He was so convinced that Hope was Lana's daughter that Jared had no doubt all of the pieces of the investigation would begin to fall into place. There would be justice for Lana. A new life would begin for the one link to her.

"Captain Rivers handled her presentation and the collection of DNA brilliantly." Mrs. Moody sat with Jared and Karin in her office after the day ended. "It was obviously a learning experience for the entire class. I have no worries regarding any repercussions. We did what was right for this child."

"Beth is a smart cop. I know that if there had been any substantial leads at the time, she would have solved this case years ago." Jared stopped and reflected on his own words. He took a deep breath as he thought about what his life might have been like if that had actually happened.

"Jared, I cannot imagine how you must feel." Mrs. Moody looked Jared squarely in the eyes. The compassion he felt was clear evidence why her career in education had been long and meaningful. "I admire your ability to view Hope as a child in need rather than as a product of the violence that was committed against your wife. It shows great strength of character."

"Mrs. Moody, you give me more credit than I deserve. I have had all of the horrible thoughts about why this child exists. To think about what my Lana endured before and after this child's birth is incomprehensible. I would give anything to be her biological father. I cannot turn back the hands of time. If it is within my power, though, I will become the father that she has always needed. Her being Lana's daughter is enough."

Up until that moment, Jared had not allowed his mind to go there. He had not consciously thought about trying to adopt Hope. Yet, his heart knew from the moment that he saw the infinity pendant. He promised to love Lana until infinity. He would do the same for her child.

As he allowed his gaze to move to Karin, he wondered what her reaction would be to his revelation. It did not surprise him to see her eyes fill with tears and her expression with understanding. The two of them could make this work. They could be a family for Hope.

Chapter Fourteen

"JARED, THANK YOU FOR COMING TO my office. I thought it would be best for you to hear the results of the test in person in case you had any questions. I'm glad that you brought Karin and your father with you."

"I figured that either way, this news is going to be hard for me to take. I need my support system." Sitting in the middle, Jared reached out and took Karin's and his father's hand in each of his own. After giving each one of them a long look and a nod, he turned back to face Beth. "We have travelled a long road, Beth. I want you to know that I appreciate everything that you have done to help me find Lana. You could have just passed the case along to one of your subordinates as you climbed the ladder. I am thankful that you have always kept Lana on your radar. I know that has made all the difference in the world."

"I appreciate that, Jared. You know that Thomas and I consider you a member of the family. Parker is convinced that you are his uncle. Since all of his real ones are far away, you are filling an important void. I'm sorry for the way you entered my life. I am thankful that you are in it."

Beth looked down at the folder in front of her. Jared had a horrible feeling that this detective, his friend, was stalling. Maybe his mind had just wanted to find Lana so badly that he imagined her in that little girl. Jared shook his head.

"No, I'm sure. I'm absolutely sure." Jared's voice was barely above a whisper.

"What did you say, Jared?" Beth looked up again.

"Nothing." He felt Karin squeeze his hand. She had heard his thoughts. Jared dared not look at her. "Go ahead and tell us what the test revealed. I'm ready."

"Okay. Here we go." Beth opened the file. "There are a lot of complicated paragraphs and charts. I'm going to skip right to the end, if that's okay with you?" Jared shook his head affirmatively. "Based on our analysis and the bio-statistical evaluation of the results, it is our determination that it is practically proven that Lana Bouvier Kennedy is the biological mother of the child herein known as Hope Doe."

There was silence in the room. Beth closed the file and looked at Jared. His eyes never left the folder as he spoke.

"So, if Lana is Hope's mother, it means that Lana is dead."

"Jared, based on what Hope has indicated, it would seem that is the logical conclusion. We can't be sure until we find a body. What this does mean is that we are going to issue a warrant for the arrest of Hope's father. Our first charge will be for abduction, with probable subsequent charges of sexual battery, assault, child endangerment, and murder."

Jared let out a long, deep breath. He felt his father's arm go around his shoulder and pull him into a silent embrace. He heard Karin choking back tears and felt a soft kiss on his cheek. He was aware of all of these things going on around him. Yet, he was numb and unable to move. Slowly, he allowed his eyes to meet Beth's as a question formed in his mind.

"It just occurred to me that I do not remember hearing Hope's last name. Maybe, I've just had a block on it all this time. What is the name of the man who you are now going to arrest?"

"Morris Dillion."

Beth uttered the name without hesitation. Jared's eyes bugged out as the realization passed over him.

"Morris Dillion. I know Morris Dillion. He used to work at my firm. I drove him home one day. He lived a block away from our house." It was not the familiar feeling of rage that began building inside of Jared. Instead it had the flavor of understanding and regret. Then, a flash of awareness occurred that made his brain feel like it might explode. "He was in the elevator that day. He heard me tell Vince my plans for our anniversary. I told him everything."

"This is why I couldn't tell you this over the phone. I did a background investigation on Hope's father the same day as the DNA test. It revealed that Dillion was working with you at the time of the abduction and for several years afterward."

"Please don't tell me that Lana was within a couple of blocks of our home the whole time."

"No. Dillion moved about a year after the abduction. The house that Hope is living in was in his late wife's family for years. He probably took her directly there." Beth closed her eyes. Jared feared she had more to say. "There's another connection. You and Lana went to college with his step-son, Roger Trey Zachmann."

"He was working with Lana around the time she got promoted." Jared's eyes darted back and forth as he thought about that name. "That's why that guy looked so familiar to me. He's the one." Jared closed his eyes as the image popped in his memory. "He's the guy that was putting the moves on Lana that first day I talked to her in class. Roger was Trey. I should have remembered. So, he was involved in the abduction, too?"

"No, he could not have been. A couple of weeks before Lana was abducted, Roger Trey Zachmann died of an overdose. That could have been the catalyst for his stepfather's actions. We won't know until we begin questioning Dillion. We may never know. But, obviously, there is a connection, and it goes back a long time."

"If we had only remembered him." Jared leaned down and put his head in his hands as a sick feeling washed over him. "I should have listened to Lana. I shouldn't have gotten out of the Jeep."

Beth rose from her desk and walked around to stand in front of Jared. He looked up at her as he stood. She drew him into an embrace.

"We are going to get this bastard, Jared. We are going to make sure that Hope is safe. Then, we are going to get him and we are going to nail him to the wall."

"IN AN INCREDIBLE turn of events, the suspected abductor of Lana Kennedy has been arrested. Channel 10 News has obtained exclusive information that an unnamed male has been arrested in the Edison Heights area. No information has been released about whether Lana Kennedy has been located. Stay tuned to Channel 10 for the latest updates."

Jared peeked through the blinds of the front window of his house. A steady rain fell causing the midday sky to look darker than normal. Down the street, Jared could see the sun shining. It created a strange surreal effect. Two television news trucks were already camped out on the street as police officers stood stoically while microphones and cameras were shoved in their faces. As he was watching, Jared saw Beth and another officer pull into his driveway. He quickly walked to the door to let them in.

"It's already a madhouse out there, and we are just getting started."

Beth took off her raincoat and hung it on the coatrack at the door. Jared paused to look at the piece of furnishing. Lana had found it at an estate sale shortly before they were married. He was not sure that he had ever seen her raincoat hang there.

"Jared, this is Officer Brent Pannell. During the next few days, as we are conducting the search of the house and grounds where Hope was living, Officer Pannell will assist me in keeping you informed. Unfortunately, I am also scheduled to be testifying in court in a murder trial this week, so my time on the search scene will be limited. Brent will be keeping both of us updated."

"Come on in, and I will get you both some coffee." Jared kept talking as the two sat down. "By all means, Beth, you go to that court and help put some murderer away. I'm counting on you to do the same for Lana. You have arrested him, right?"

"Yes, Jared. Morris Dillion is in custody. I was there myself when the warrant was served. The man was in shock. He did not resist at all. I think that he could not believe that he had been caught."

"And Hope? She is okay?"

"Yes, she is safe and placed in foster care." Beth put both of her hands around the mug of coffee that Jared handed her. "I know that sounds scary, but she is with a wonderful foster family. They have experience caring for children who have been through extreme trauma."

"Hope being in foster care does not concern me at all. Any place is far better than where she was and who she was with. She's already proven what a strong and brave girl she is. Her mother would be proud." Jared lowered his head and pondered what he had said. "Calling Lana Hope's mother is still hard for me. It just doesn't seem real that Lana could have had a child without me."

"Jared, the days ahead are not going to get easier." Officer Pannell finally spoke. "You may think that since the abductor has been apprehended everything will be better. The search of the house and grounds will, no doubt, reveal some horrid things, possibly including the remains of your wife. This will get worse before it gets better."

"I appreciate your words. After I figured out who I thought Hope was, I started to accept that my wife would not be coming home. Unless that little girl just imagined seeing her mother dead, Lana is gone and has been for a while. It is the last thing I ever wanted to find out. But, now, I have a new mission and that involves taking care of her daughter. For me, that really can't begin until the monster who stole my wife is convicted, behind bars, or worse. I don't want him to ever breathe the same air as Hope again. I don't even want him in the same zip code with her. Anything less than that is unacceptable. I have a message for the forensics team. Will you deliver it for me, Officer Pannell?"

"Yes, sir."

"You tell them that I expect the search to cover every millimeter of that property with a fine tooth comb. I want them to find every speck of evidence possible so that piece of scum can be put into prison forever. It's time for Lana to rest. I need for you to find the love of my life so that she can rest in peace. Then, I will spend the rest of my life making sure that her daughter is happy, healthy, and safe."

THE FOLLOWING DAYS were a whirlwind of activity. Each day brought new information as the search of the house and grounds where Hope lived continued. Beth Rivers and the other detectives discouraged him from getting near the scene. Despite the warning, Jared spent the first two days of the search making loops through the neighborhood, getting as close as he could get without tipping off the media of his presence. He could feel an urgency surrounding it as investigators and forensic technicians worked night and day. The house was almost an eyesore in the neighborhood, so out of place that it almost disappeared. At least a hundred years old, it was huge by today's standards, spanning five stories from basement to attic.

As the sun was beginning to set on the second day of the search, Jared brought Karin with him as he slowly drove as near as he dared.

"Didn't this house ever seem unusual to you when you used to bring Hope home from her afternoons with you?" Jared slumped down a little in the driver's seat as a cameraman got out of a news truck that was diagonally parked across the street from them. "It looks like something out of a horror movie."

"It looks that way to you now because of what you know has occurred here." Karin reached for Jared's hand. "It would not look the same to you if you were just driving by. It would look like a big, old, slightly neglected house. A house that probably holds a history decades in the making."

"All I can see are bars on the windows. All I can hear is Lana's screams of frustration. I can't believe how close this house was the whole time. After all those initial years of searching and no concrete leads of anyone seeing Lana in the area, I assumed that she had been taken somewhere far away."

Jared and Karin were silent for a moment as they watched the activity going on outside the house. By looking between several news trucks that were hovering just past the yellow caution tape, Jared could see forensics technicians going back and forth on the porch of the house while others were digging in various points in the yard.

"It is nerve wracking being here and not being able to participate in the search." Jared raised his hand as Karin started to speak. "I know that I would be nothing but trouble over there. It still doesn't change the fact that I feel helpless." Jared took in a deep breath. He took his gaze off of the house and focused on Karin for a moment. "Who knows how long Lana spent inside of that place? I can't imagine that he would have let her out. She was so smart and resourceful. If he had taken her anywhere, she would have found a way to communicate with someone."

"Jared, you've got to let your mind relax and accept what is now happening. You can't dwell on what happened all those years she was missing. It will drive you crazy."

"It already has. The strangest thing to me now though is not what they are going to find in there. What is tugging at my heart is the vision of the little girl who lived there. This precious little child who came into this world in captivity and had no idea that her mother was the most wonderful woman on Earth and that her father is a monster beyond description."

"I believe that Hope knew some of both of those things."

"Perhaps, but what is most heart wrenching to me is that she is now sitting in a house with strangers and she feels more secure with them than she may have felt at any point in her entire life. I should be focused on the prospect of finally knowing what happened to my Lana, on the miniscule fragment of possibility that she could somehow be alive. I've spent almost the last decade living and breathing that hope. Now, all my heart can think about is that sweet child who didn't appreciate my penguin jokes and loves ice cream."

"That same little girl feels a connection to you and a trust in you deep within her soul. A connection that was no doubt genetically willed to her by her wonderful mother, knowing that one day her daughter would have to call upon her instincts to open her heart and be found. You can talk all you want to about finding Hope, Jared. The truth of the matter is that she found you." Jared had looked back at the house for a moment as Karin spoke. He felt her hand on his chin, pulling his attention back to her. "Are you hearing me? Several of her previous teachers and I all agree. Hope had been around class parents, chaperones on field trips, and other guests in the classrooms. No one remembers her ever interacting with any of them, even when spoken to. She would politely answer and 'make herself small,' as one teacher put it. Hope made herself big when you came along. There was something that drew you to her."

"It was Lana. On some level, I could sense Lana's spirit in Hope. Thankfully, Lana's genetics beat out that monster's. I don't even consider him a part of Hope. I don't see any of that in her. She's all her mother. I am so happy that we were able to get the genetic testing done without his knowledge. I feel sure that he would have either taken Hope away somewhere, or worse."

"I think the worst was a real possibility. I'm not really sure how Hope has survived this long."

"There are so many unanswered questions. They may never be resolved. I just hope that I can get custody of her. I know I haven't really talked to you about this and it's not fair for me to assume—"

"Assume what? Assume that I do not already love Hope? Assume that I do not want to be in your life? Jared, I think we are past that. I love you. I would be honored to raise this incredible child with you. I don't care what her genetics say. I know who her real father is."

An overwhelming urge to kiss Karin came over Jared. An urge that he decided he should act on. Just as their lips were about to meet, there was a knock on Jared's window. He gave Karin a wide-eyed look as he spoke.

"Please tell me that it is not a reporter."

"It is not a reporter." Karin sat back in her seat. "We might be arrested."

Jared watched a smirk cross Karin's face before he turned and began to roll the window down.

"Yes, officer. How can I help you?"

"Mr. Kennedy, Officer Pannell would like for you to vacate the premises, sir."

"I was just driving by."

"Yes, sir. We have seen you drive by numerous times over the last couple of days. I believe that Captain Rivers and Officer Pannell specifically asked for you not to visit this area. This is a crime scene, sir. It is not appropriate for a family member to be here during our investigation. Do you understand, Mr. Kennedy?"

"Yes, I understand. It's just hard, knowing—"

"Sir, no one doubts how difficult this is for you. I cannot imagine how you feel. Quite frankly, I hope I never understand how you feel. Let us do our jobs so that we can put that scumbag away for a very long time."

Jared nodded and started his vehicle as the officer began to walk away. As Jared pulled the car from the curb, the sun began to fully set behind the house. The light gave the illusion of a fire beginning to consume it. It would be an appropriate end—a closure—to a structure that was truly a prison cell. It was not time yet for the end. It was only the beginning—the beginning of a story that already had an ending.

Chapter Fifteen

JARED KNEW WHEN THE PHONE RANG. It was like a breeze passed through the room, barely touching his skin. It was like a whisper with no voice. Picking up the phone, he spoke the words before even saying hello.

"They've found her."

"Jared, how? Who called you?" Beth River's voice was tinged with concern and aggravation. "I specifically told Officer Pannell and the team that I would be—"

"This is the first call I have received. I just know." Jared doubled over as the realization began to hit him. A shooting pain started at the core of his chest, the place where his heart used to be. "Where did they find her?"

"We are not a hundred percent sure yet that it is her. There will have to be forensics tests to verify—"

"Where did they find her?" Jared repeated his question as in one swift movement he rose back up. The sharp pain left his chest and shot into the center of his skull. "It's her. She's there."

"It was the backyard under a concrete slab that looked like the foundation of an old outbuilding."

"Was it a decent grave?"

"Jared, I really don't think we need to be talking about—"

"Was she buried decently?" Jared could feel the rage growing inside of him. "It's all going to come out. Don't make me hear the description on the evening news, Beth. I can take it. I have to know."

There was silence on the other end of the phone. Jared could almost hear the anguish that Beth was feeling.

"I'm coming over."

"I THINK WHEN we get to the end of our lives we begin to see everything in Polaroids."

Jared talked to himself as he prepared a pot of coffee while he was waiting for Beth to arrive. He placed the pot on the dining room table, next to a bottle of scotch. He really did not consider himself to be a drinker. But he had bought that particular bottle several years ago for the conversation that was about to occur.

As if on cue or by some sensory radar that parents have, Jared's father arrived right ahead of Beth. It was not even nine o'clock in the morning, when through Jared's kitchen door walked Cary Kennedy carrying a bakery box.

"How you doing this morning, son?" Despite Jared's suspicions, his father's demeanor did not reveal that he had any knowledge of what was about to occur. "Since when do you drink scotch in your morning coffee?" Mr. Kennedy looked from the table to Jared.

"I think you may want to join me. You didn't get any phone calls from Beth this morning?"

"No. From Beth Rivers? No. What's going on?" Mr. Kennedy slowly sat down in one of the dining room chairs. Jared could almost see his father's hair becoming grayer. He wondered how many silver streaks his own hair would have after today. "I just felt like I needed to come over here this morning. Something told me to stop at the bakery, get some chocolate croissants, and come see my son."

"Sweet Bites on Wilkerson Drive?"

"Yes, how did you—"

Jared rubbed his forehead as a new pain shot through it simultaneously as the doorbell rang.

"That's Beth, Dad. They have found Lana."

Before his father could respond, Jared walked toward the front door. As he opened it, Jared took a good look at Beth Rivers. He had never really noticed how small the woman was. In the years he had known her, she had risen in the ranks of the police department and always carried herself with an air of authority and strength in any situation. She was a large person in her demeanor, who he often thought filled the room with her strong presence. In his doorway that morning, the slump in her shoulders, the tiredness in her eyes, made Beth look very small.

"Jared."

"You must have been driving when you called."

"Yes, I have an officer with me outside. We are going to up our security around your home as the news is released regarding our discovery." Beth walked into the dining room where Jared's father was still sitting. Jared noticed that the faraway look on his father's face mirrored the feelings that Jared had inside. "Hello, Mr. Kennedy."

"Hello, Beth." Jared's father snapped out of his haze and nodded.

"I see you all were about to have breakfast." Beth pointed to the coffee, scotch, and pastry as she sat down. "Looks a lot like a cop's dinner after a long hard night."

"Help yourself to whatever you want. I'm ready to hear what you've got tell us."

Beth gave Jared a long look before she began to speak. He thought back to the first time he had met her as she interviewed him from beside his hospital bed.

"As I said on the phone, remains were found under a concrete slab in the backyard." Jared heard his father gasp, but he chose to not look in his direction. "It looked like what might have been the foundation of an old outbuilding."

"No real grave, she was just tossed aside, disposed."

"Hidden is more likely. He had obviously been successful in keeping her secure in that house or another location for many years. When something went wrong, he could not draw attention to the situation."

"Something went wrong? What do you mean?"

"It will take lots of testing and investigating, but what Hope told you and Karin seems to make sense if these remains are indeed Lana."

"She said that she found her mother in the basement."

"And that her mother had a gash in her head. The preliminary evaluation of the remains shows similar results."

Suddenly, Jared felt a clutching in his chest. It was not like an anxiety attack. He had too many of those over the last few years. The feeling began deep inside his heart, at its very core. It was as if the beginning of him, his very existence, was breaking in one piercing moment.

"This is the end of infinity." The words were clear and crisp coming out of his mouth. He could not understand how they had formed, yet he heard them just the same. "Our love was until infinity. This is the moment that my soul begins to die." Jared stood up.

"Son. Son, I'm here, Jared." Mr. Kennedy rose to walk toward Jared. "I understand your grief. We will work through this together."

"No, Dad. We will not. Your grief was yours and this is mine. Mom left you because of a horrible disease that attacked her body. You had a chance to be there with her during her final weeks and hours. You never worried about where she was. She never left your sight. You got to say goodbye."

"I'm sorry, son. I just want to help you."

"This monster tracked us like animals. He stole her in the dark of night. He held her captive and did God knows what to her within the bars of the prison he created for her. Years and years passed. Now, I find out that he even disposed of her like trash in the backyard." Jared clutched his chest again. "I promised to love her until infinity. What else do I have without that?"

Everything around Jared became blurry, and then, darkness.

Chapter Sixteen

"Wake up, Mr. Jared. Open your eyes."

The voice seemed to be coming from a great distance. It sounded vaguely familiar.

"Isn't he going to open his eyes? Doesn't he want to see me?"

Jared's mind raced as he tried to remember where he was and what was happening.

"He is very tired. He might need to sleep some more."

He recognized that voice. It was Karin. His memory returned. He was at her apartment.

"I don't see why he has to be sleeping while I am here."

A smile crossed his lips. He could have sworn that was the voice of—

"Maybe we should go back into the kitchen and have a snack. Perhaps, he will wake in up a little while."

Jared heard a loud sigh come from the location where the other voice had been.

"Don't let her eat all of the ice cream." Jared opened his eyes as he spoke and saw a small face turn in his direction. A smile crossed her face—a real smile.

"Mr. Jared, you're awake. I've got so much to tell you." Hope rushed back to Jared's bed and touched the comforter that he was under. "I live in a different house with new people. And guess what they have?" Hope's eyes were big as she awaited his answer.

"A penguin." Jared slowly raised himself up. His head felt like he had been medicated for a long time. "A penguin in a tuxedo."

"No." Hope let out a small giggle. "You are so funny. Penguins don't live in houses."

"Not even ice houses?" Jared looked around the room. Karin was standing near the doorway. His father was sitting in a chair in the corner.

"Only in documentaries." Hope hopped up on the bed and sat next to Jared. "My new family has a dog."

New family. A scowl replaced the smile that had formed on Jared's face. He tried not to let it show.

"What kind of dog is it?"

"It's a big one." Hope shook her head as Jared looked at her. "It's almost as tall as me."

"Does this dog have a name?"

"Yes, his name is Buster. He's very hairy."

"Dogs are like that."

"Hope was worried about you, so she asked if she could come and see you. I told her that she had to wait until you got out of the hospital." Karin's eyes locked with Jared's. He noticed there were dark circles under them. She looked like she had not gotten much rest. "Beth brought her by about an hour ago."

"You remember her, don't you, Mr. Jared? She's the police officer who came to my class. I think she found my Mommie."

Jared's eyes grew big as Hope spoke. His peripheral vision detected some movement in the doorway. He turned to see Beth enter the room.

"Remember what I told you about that, Hope?" Beth made eye contact with Jared.

"They have to do tests to make sure." Hope leaned over and whispered to Jared. "But I know it is my Mommie."

Jared closed his eyes as the pain returned to his chest. He had to fight it. Hope must have noticed his expression. He felt her small hand on top of his.

"It's okay, Mr. Jared. My Mommie is at peace now. She told me that if she ever went away, I had to remember that she didn't have a choice. She wouldn't leave me on purpose." Jared's eyes filled with tears. "But, she said that I had to be a big girl and remember that she was at peace and that she would love me wherever she was, until infinity, like my necklace."

Jared watched as Hope pulled the pendant out from underneath her shirt. He tried to swallow the lump in his throat, but a sob still escaped. He turned away so that Hope could not see his face.

"Let's go get those bowls of ice cream ready while Miss Beth talks to Jared for a few minutes."

Hope lifted her small hand away from Jared's as she got down off of the bed. That small gentle act caused a feeling to rise in Jared unlike any he had ever experienced. He longed to reach out and pull the child back to him and engulf her in a hug. He could not be sure if it was her love for her mother that incited the emotion or if he had begun to allow himself to really care for the child she had left behind. He managed to wipe the tears from his face as he watched her follow Karin. Hope turned back and looked at him before she crossed the doorway. Her recent happy face had turned to one of worry.

"It's incredible, isn't it?" Beth sat down in the chair opposite Jared's father.

"Incredible? You are going to have to explain what you mean, Beth, my head is pretty fuzzy."

"It's no wonder with the strong meds you were given in the hospital."

"Why was I on meds? What happened to me?"

"You almost had a heart attack, son. There's some long medical name for it. I can't remember."

"When I came to your house after we had found Lana's remains, you all of a sudden clutched your chest and blacked out. We rushed you to the hospital. Given the situation, the doctors first thought you were having a severe panic attack. They later determined it was a little more serious than that."

Jared started to stand up and felt a little light-headed. He watched as his father rubbed his brow with a concerned look on his face.

"Okay. What was wrong?"

"You have broken heart syndrome."

"I've had that for a lot of years now." Jared tried to stand again. This time he was more successful. He walked into the bathroom that was adjacent to the bedroom.

"No, Jared, I'm serious. Broken heart syndrome is an actual medical condition. The cardiologist explained to me that it is often caused by an extreme stressful situation, especially one that is sudden. Your father is right that there are a couple of other long names for the condition, but it is basically a temporary disruption of your heart's normal pumping function in one area of the heart. The rest of the heart usually continues to function normally but with more forceful contractions. When a person has a stressful situation occur, this condition can be caused by the heart's reaction to a surge of stress hormones."

"What you had to tell me wasn't exactly a shock; I have been expecting this news." Jared looked at himself in the mirror after splashing cool water on his face. He wondered where the gray hair had come from and when he had shaved last. "I should have had that reaction when Lana was taken."

"The doctor thinks you probably did." Mr. Kennedy responded as Jared walked back into the room. "He looked at your records from when you were attacked. There was evidence that this probably happened before."

"Still, why now?"

"I think the surge of emotions that you were experiencing the other day were probably more apparent to us than to you. We could see it on your face. It was the shock of the finality of it. That coupled with all of the positive, but confused, emotions you have about that little girl in there. Hope is an amazing child. That's what I was talking about when she first left the room. Her transformation over the last week has been just incredible."

"Yeah, I heard how she referred to the people she is staying with as her new family." After tucking his shirt into his pants, Jared combed his hair. "I'm glad that there are good people taking care of her. I wonder if the courts will want to award custody to them."

"Jared, don't jump the gun. The Herrings are experienced foster care providers. They are a strong family unit with a teenage daughter and college-age son. They have taken care of many children who have come from traumatic situations, including several who have lost a parent violently or suffered abuse themselves. These folks specialize in providing a stable and nurturing environment for the children to begin to learn what normal is. It is a powerfully important transitionary experience for the children to later be adopted. The Herrings do not adopt, they foster."

A feeling of relief passed over Jared. He did not realize how afraid he was of losing Hope. He was afraid that it would be like losing Lana all over again.

"You heard her say that I helped find her mother. I've been to visit Hope three times in the last week. Donna Herring thought it would be good for Hope to be able to get out any questions she might have. I was amazed how much that Hope knew about the situation. She understood that her father was arrested. She thinks it is solely because of her mother's death. At this point, she does not know how her mother came to be in that house."

"Had they been there all along?"

"It appears so. This house was in the family for about one hundred years. Apparently it sat empty for a couple of decades before Roger Trey Zachmann's mother inherited it about twenty years ago. She died shortly thereafter, leaving the house to her only son. He moved into it about ten years ago. After he died, it went to Morris Dillion, his stepfather. Dillion says that he brought Lana there that very night that he abducted her. He did not live there himself until after Hope was born."

"So, he's—"

"Mr. Jared, your ice cream is melting." All eyes turned

toward the doorway as Hope ran into the room. "You better hurry."

"Okay. I will." Jared smiled as Beth stood up to follow Hope out. "I'll be right there."

"We can continue this conversation tomorrow. If you are feeling up to it, you can come by my office in the morning. There's a lot to talk about."

As Beth left the room with Hope, Mr. Kennedy stood up and began to exit.

"You talk about infinity, son. There's your infinity."

"Dad, remember in this situation, just because she is Lana's child doesn't make her mine."

"Are you going to let a little thing like genetics stand in your way? I thought you vowed to love Lana forever."

"I did, Dad. I will."

"Well, son, she just walked out of the room. Her mother's dead and her father might as well be. Lana needs you more than ever. She needs you to be there for her daughter. Like she always vowed, Lana's giving you infinity. You better take it."

"YOU LOOK BETTER this morning, Jared. Perhaps, it was that extra-large serving of ice cream you consumed yesterday afternoon." Beth set a cup of coffee on her desk in front of Jared. "I'm glad that Karin and Mr. Kennedy came with you this morning. It is good for everyone to hear these details together." Jared turned and smiled at Karin and his father seated behind him.

"Perhaps, it was the server who was the best medicine." As Beth had told him, Jared was amazed at the change that occurred in Hope's temperament after just a few days in a new environment. "Hope was a chatterbox."

"It's one of the things that amazes me the most about this job. I have seen children come out of horrendous and terrifying situations. Of course, they carry those physical and emotional scars with them for the rest of their lives. Yet, given a little love, discipline, and attention, kids are resilient to bounce back and begin functioning normally, much quicker than adults do."

"It's wonderful. I'm working to overcome emotional challenges myself. Please continue to tell me about Hope's questions last night. What does she know and understand about the situation?"

"Good place to start. I told you that we arrested Morris Dillion while Hope was in school. That, of course, prevented him from taking her somewhere or harming her. So, she was not removed from the home. She was simply taken directly from school to foster care. Mrs. Moody accompanied her as she was acquainted with the Herrings from previous students they fostered."

"I'm glad she had Mrs. Moody with her."

"Mrs. Moody helped the child protection services staff explain to Hope what was happening. As I understand, Hope remained very calm and unemotional. She had two questions and a request. Hope asked if she ever had to go back there and if someone would look for her mother in the backyard."

Jared closed his eyes and let out a deep breath. He felt incredible sadness mixed with fiery anger building inside him.

"Hope told us where her mother was located. She watched Dillion pour the concrete slab."

"This is like a bad movie." Jared rose and began to pace.

"Unfortunately, Jared, this is not. This is a reality of our society that thankfully most people don't have to experience. I will tell you that the worst things you read in fiction or see in movies are probably not nearly as bad as real life can be." Beth picked up her beeping cell phone and ignored the call. "But the flip side of that are little adults like Hope. She had a strong mother who decided the best thing she could do for her child was help her develop a wall of strength around her. It has served Hope well."

Jared stopped pacing for a moment as he thought about what Beth said. He had no doubt that Lana carefully considered the best way to prepare her daughter for survival. Keeping Hope safe and ready to handle whatever came next would have been her focus.

"You said that Hope asked for something. What was it?"

"She wanted to know if we could retrieve one of her toys. Of course, one of our officers immediately did that."

Jared nodded as he sat back down and attempted to drink the now cold coffee.

"Because of the information that Hope gave us, the discovery of the remains did not take as long as it might have. Since we already had verified information regarding Lana's DNA, the matching of it with the remains was relatively quick and simple." Beth took a deep breath and looked Jared straight in the eye. "I can confirm that the remains we found were that of Lana Bouvier Kennedy."

The words were spoken. It was final. Unlike a few days earlier, there was not a piercing pain in his chest, he did not feel as if he could not breathe, nor did he feel the urge to break something. For the first time in more years than he wanted to count, he felt peace. Jared knew that it was because now he had a new focus, a dual one—justice for the love of his life and security for the future of her daughter.

"How soon can the trial begin?"

"Hold on, Jared. There's more information that I need to share with you. I'm glad to see that you are calmer, and you don't appear to be having any of the heart symptoms that you did the other day. But you must brace yourself as there are more details to share." Beth opened up a file folder on her desk. Jared saw lines of worry form on her forehead. "I'm not going to go into all the details right now regarding the condition of the remains. I know that you think you want to know, but I believe you should process what you have already heard first. You will hear these details too many times once the trail begins."

Jared nodded and reached his right hand across the desk to Beth. The detective grasped it and their eyes locked for a moment.

"Beth, I want you to know that I appreciate everything you have done on this case. I know that it lay dormant for many years, and it was difficult for you to make it a priority. Somehow, I think that you always did. I will be eternally grateful."

"Jared, I could tell you that I was just doing my job. It would not be true. I decided a long time ago that I was going to do everything in my power to find your wife, and I was going to do it because of Lana. I am Lana. My sister is Lana. The lady who rings up my groceries is Lana. We are all women who, through no fault of our own, in the blink of an eye could become the victim of someone like Morris Dillion. We are going to put this guy away, and he will never hurt another person again."

Jared fought back the emotion that was rising in him as he briefly squeezed Beth's hand before releasing it. He leaned back into his chair and waited for her to continue.

"After the remains were transported to the coroner's office is when the real work could begin to piece together how Lana's life ended. We are quite fortunate to have a highly experienced medical examiner at our disposable.

Dr. Brenda Brindell came to us from a major metropolitan hospital on the West Coast. Dr. Brindell grew up here and returned about a decade ago to care for her aging parents. Her career consisted of being used repeatedly as an expert witness in more homicide cases each month than we have here in a year. Her experience is vast, and she is known for her thoroughness and attention to detail. We can speculate that even the general evidence would make this an open-and-shut case; you've seen enough high profile cases in the media in recent years to understand that is not always the way it turns out. Having her expertise can make all the difference in seeing that justice is carried out."

"I have met Dr. Brindell. I am more acquainted with her husband, Murray. My firm handles their investment portfolio."

"Small world, isn't it?" Beth shuffled through some papers in the file in front of her. "As Dr. Brindell was examining the remains, it surprised her that some of Lana's clothing was still well intact. Her examination of the clothing found a piece of paper inside the lining of her bra. It was in a tiny plastic bag. The note was folded many times. Creases indicated that it had been in its hiding place for many years. Miraculously, the note could still be read."

"What did the note say?" Jared's voice trembled as his mind raced with the knowledge that this was a message from Lana—a direct link to her thoughts before she died. An emotion crossed over him unlike any he had ever felt.

"It was one simple sentence, clearly written in block letters. 'The secret is more than I can bear.' Does this mean anything to you, Jared?"

A scowl formed on Jared's face as he searched his memory for any recollection. The words themselves did not hold any special meaning to him.

"They do not. I cannot think of anything in my life with Lana that they would refer to. Do you think it was the secret of Hope's existence? The secret that this horrible human who took Lana away also fathered this precious child. Like any person, I know Lana would be conflicted with how Hope had come into her life."

"I thought that at first, Jared. Then, I remembered that you had told me how brilliant Lana was. How her mind could work in complex ways and break things down into simpler components. Something inside me said that this was a message—a code to help us find something even more important. I lay awake that night after I first saw the note. I rolled the words over and over in my mind a thousand times. Then, it hit me."

"Hope's bear."

Jared turned around so quickly, he almost gave himself whiplash. He had forgotten that Karin was sitting right behind him with his father. Her quiet and strong voice brought him back to his own reality—a life that included her.

"You know about it." Beth smiled as Karin met her gaze. "You knew Hope had a special teddy bear."

"Oh, yes, all the teachers know about Hope's bear. We could gauge her emotions by it. She would have weeks where she would seem fine, almost like any other child. Then she would show up with the bear, and we knew that emotionally, or lack thereof, she was in bad shape. It is not unusual for a child to have some security item. It is not unusual for the item to almost have a personality to those who observe the child with it." Jared was now turned around in his chair facing Karin. She paused and reached for his hand. "I always thought that, perhaps, the bear represented Hope's mother to her."

"I believe that you are right. One of the officers had remembered that Hope had only asked for one toy to be recovered from her home after her father was arrested. It was a teddy bear. Karin, do you know what the bear's name is?"

"I do. It just hit me. It never occurred to me before." Jared searched Karin's eyes for meaning. "The bear's name is Ken."

"Yes, she calls him Ken. Hope says that she shortened his name. Her mother named the bear. His name is Kennedy."

Jared's body began to shake as he choked back tears. His vision became blurred as his eyes were pooling with water. Beth continued talking.

"So, I went to see Hope at the Herring home." Beth sat down in front of Jared. "As I have already mentioned, she is getting excellent care. The family has experience working with children who have had seriously traumatic childhoods. Each time I have been there, she has asked me if she has to go back to 'that house.' Each time, I assured her that she never had to go back there again. The last time, I think I heard a giggle."

"It's just amazing." Jared wiped the tears from his eyes and smiled.

"I had a theory that maybe there was a secret hiding place inside of Hope's bear. I thought that maybe Lana knew that Dillion would not mess with Hope's favorite toy. I asked Hope if I could see Ken. I had pre-arranged for the foster mother to distract Hope for a few minutes and get her out of the room. They took her into the kitchen to get something to drink. So, I started examining the bear and, sure enough, there was a little flap under Ken's shirt that held another note. Again, it was folded many times and was inside a little plastic bag."

Jared watched as Beth pulled the note out of the file. It seemed like an eternity as she took it out of the bag and carefully unfolded it before holding it out to him. Jared shook his head.

"No, I can't do it. I can't. You read it. Read it out loud. You already know its contents. Everyone else in this room deserves to know. My hands could not hold the paper. My eyes could not focus on her words. My only hope—" Jared's voice broke as he heard his own words. "My only hope is that my ears shall allow me the gift to hear her voice as you read it."

Beth shook her head affirmatively and brought the note back in front of her. Taking a deep breath as her eyes met Jared's, she began to read.

If you have found this, I am certainly dead. I pray that my beautiful daughter has survived this imprisoned life and has found peace and happiness on the other side of these walls. Hope is the only thing that keeps me going. Perhaps that is why I gave her this name. The dual meaning does not escape me, even in this shaky state of sanity in which I dwell.

I could have ended our lives, she and I, long ago. Our captor is not as smart as he claims. He's given me the tools, in the guise of ordinary tasks, to free us from this inhumane life. Perhaps he knows that I could never do it because she is my link to the life he took from me. She is my *infinity.*

I leave this note so that one day maybe a miracle will occur and my child will be free. She was born seven months after I was taken, in the early morning hours of May 14. He brought someone here to help me—a woman to whom I will be eternally grateful. The fear in her eyes told me that she would not be able to free me. Yet, her gift to me was priceless as I needed the courage to push my child into this horrid world that I found myself in. My precious baby needed help to breathe her first breaths. Whatever birth certificate was created to give her passage into civilized life is a false one. She needs to know who she is and who she is not. This man who took my life is not her father. Her father is out there somewhere dying of a broken heart, searching for a face he will never see again. Her name is Hope Infinity Kennedy.

Her mother is Lana Bouvier Kennedy. Her father is Jared Michael Kennedy. Please help her find her father. I never had the chance that fateful night to tell him of her impending arrival. I am sure that he loves her without knowing of her existence. My heart has told his heart that she belongs to him. I have faith that somehow he will find her and love her until infinity, as I have loved him.

Jared heard a scream. It seemed far away from him. Too far to be coming from his own mouth as it was. It was pain, excruciating pain, mixed with joy unlike he had ever known. His heart would now surely break from the shock had it not already done so all those years ago. It only had one choice now—it had to begin to heal.

Epilogue

IT WAS THE TWENTY-FIFTH ANNIVERSARY of their first date. His life had come full circle as he waited on a bench under a tree for his daughter on the very campus where he had met her mother. Jared turned around and fingered the bronze plate that adorned the bench. He had it placed under the tree in Lana's honor nearly fifteen years earlier. Jared never imagined that he would one day sit there waiting on their daughter to get out of class. It seemed like a dream. He had awakened from a nightmare to find there was a beautiful world full of hope on the other side. Hope. His hope. Her hope. Their hope.

His life had changed so much in the years since he found Hope. Jared and Karin had married shortly thereafter and Karin had adopted Hope. A few years later, a son had joined their family. Zachary was ten and adored his older sister. This life was more wonderful than he ever imagined was possible.

"Hey, Dad. Have you been waiting long?" Hope appeared in front of him, interrupting his thoughts. "My lab partner was late, and we were the last ones to finish the assignment."

"I didn't mind. It's peaceful here, relaxing."

Jared paused and looked deeply into the eyes of his daughter. It was the one aspect of her that he recognized as pure him. Her natural beauty, so casual and carefree, was all Lana. The look of wonder or serious thought that came from her deep blue eyes was his contribution to her miraculous creation.

"Sit down here a minute before we go. Let's talk."

Hope put her backpack on the ground and sat down on the bench next to her father. A student passed by and said hello to her, causing Hope to smile and wave. Jared choked back tears that formed in his throat. It was so like his college days with the young girl who would become Hope's mother. It was like a momentary flashback in time.

"What do you want to talk about, Dad?"

Dad. It was such a simple word. The power behind it so immense. Her existence had been a secret to him for years. It was an illusion that he only dreamed to be part of, that was a reality he almost completely missed.

"I remember a moment many years ago when I thought my life was over."

"Yeah, the night that Mom was taken." A sad expression appeared where the smile had been.

"It was a horrible night. You are old enough to understand this now. As time passed, I realized that my life with her was over. At the time, that meant to me that my life was over."

"You loved her that much."

"I loved her more than that. I loved her more than my own life. I loved her until infinity." Jared watched as Hope's hand automatically rose to the pendant around her neck. "So, I thought that if her life was gone, mine was gone, too." Jared paused and took his gaze from his daughter to the large lawn that extended in front of them. Dozens of people walked in different directions. "Then, I found you. Lana's life was not over because you existed. She would live on in you. Then, I found out that you were mine. In that moment, I was reborn. My life must continue. Because my life had hope. I thought the deepest truest love I would ever experience was my love for your mother. I was wrong. It was you. You are us. You are our infinity.

ACKNOWLEDGEMENTS

Writing is a glimpse inside a person's heart. It reveals the depths of a person's imagination. Few, if any, writers put words on paper perfectly from the first draft. It is a profession that requires critiquing. I am blessed to have four strong and talented women who are the first ones to read my words and offer their thoughts on how I can improve my story. These four talented and caring women are: Carole Bybee, Pam Newberry, Marcella Taylor, and Donna Stroupe. This book would not exist without them. I am grateful to call them my editors and friends.

The wonderful cover for this book was the inspiration for this story. The minute I saw this incredible design, a story idea came to me. I am grateful to the creator of it, Cassy Roop of Pink Ink Designs www.pinkindesigns.com, for providing me with the image that sparked the idea. Her talented fingers are also behind the formatting.

Many thanks to every person who takes the time and spends the money the read one of my stories. Without you, these voices would stay in my head. I am grateful for the opportunity to share them with you.

ABOUT THE AUTHOR

Rosa Lee Jude began creating her own imaginary worlds at an early age. While her career path has included stints in journalism, marketing, hospitality & tourism and local government, she is most at home at a keyboard spinning yarns of fiction and creative non-fiction. She lives in the beautiful mountains of Southwest Virginia with her patient husband and very spoiled rescue dog. Learn more about her other books and writing journey at RosaLeeJude.com.